"We may consider ourselves friends, may we not, Miss Minster?"

Sir Richard led her into the inn as he spoke.

Dorcas answered cautiously but honestly. "I would be honoured, Sir."

There was much sound of activity in the back regions, but no one was about in the hall. Sir Richard eyed the kissing-bunch as Miss Minster removed her bonnet, and he said, "Er—Miss Minster?"

"Yes?"

He advanced to a suitable position and said, "Would you mind coming here a moment?"

She walked over to him, looking enquiring and a trifle puzzled. He flicked a glance upwards, and she followed it and saw the kissing-bunch a fraction too late, for he took her by the shoulders and gently kissed her lips.

"Happy Christmas, m'dear!"

"Sir!" said Dorcas. "You should not have."

"Why not?" answered Sir Richard equably. "We have just cried friends, have we not?"

Dorcas could only nod. Her heart was beating too fast to answer.

Books by Dinah Dean

HARLEQUIN REGENCY ROMANCE
11–THE COUNTRY GENTLEMAN

HARLEQUIN HISTORICAL ROMANCE
3–THE COUNTRY COUSINS

THE COCKERMOUTH MAIL
DINAH DEAN

Harlequin Books

TORONTO • NEW YORK • LONDON
AMSTERDAM • PARIS • SYDNEY • HAMBURG
STOCKHOLM • ATHENS • TOKYO • MILAN

To the postmen of
Waltham Abbey

Original hardcover edition published in 1982 by
Mills & Boon Limited.

Harlequin Regency Romance edition published August 1989

ISBN 0-373-31107-9

Printed in U.S.A.

CHAPTER ONE

THE DECEMBER DAWN had not long broken when the cross-mail for Cockermouth left the stones of Kendal, passed through the toll-gate, and swung northwestwards towards the grey fells which loomed in the distance, patched with the gold of dead bracken and netted by drystone walls. Overhead the sky was pale blue between billowing clouds dyed in strange shades of grey, gold and pink, but over the fells the clouds massed more thickly and were ominously leaden in hue.

There were no outside passengers on the coach. The dragsman sat easily on his box, the many capes of his thick driving-coat hunched about his ears and his white beaver-hat rammed down almost to his eyebrows, with little visible between but a swathing of knitted muffler through which he occasionally whistled reedily to encourage his two pair of cattle in their steady trot. The guard, a wiry little fellow cocooned in waistcoats and mufflers inside his greatcoat, carefully checked his waybill and time-sheet, beating his gloved hands alternately against his thighs to knock some life into his fingers.

Five passengers rode inside, jerking and swaying as the vehicle lurched along the uneven road. The offside corner facing forward was occupied by Miss Dorcas Minster, a young lady not very far past twenty, whose pale oval face held an expression of calm composure at odds with the apprehensive look which became noticeable in her eyes when there was nothing to distract her from her thoughts. Her feet were numbed with cold inside her patched boots, her plain dark woollen dress and redingote were four years behind the fashion, and her cloak, which had seemed so thick and warm, considering its comparatively low price, when she bought it two years ago, felt paper-thin in the bitter weather. Her bonnet was small and plain, and her carefully-darned gloves knitted. She held her reticule tightly in both hands, the chain handle twisted round her wrist, for it held her entire fortune—fourteen shillings and three-pence.

Diagonally opposite her lounged a tall, lean, broadshouldered man in a well-worn heavy coat lined with rabbit fur. He wore a fur cap pulled well down over his forehead, with earflaps which framed his lantern jaw most unbecomingly. At breakfast that morning, when this little group first met, he had introduced himself curtly as "Fred'rick Petts" in the unmistakable accents of a Londoner, adding no further information, and seemed rather out of place in the Lake District in midwinter. At present, his eyes were shut and he appeared to be asleep.

The other nearside passenger was his opposite in every way, being short, stout, nearer sixty than fifty, and given to delivering somewhat pedantic dissertations with all the authority to be expected of one of his profession, for he had announced himself to be James Tupper, solicitor, of Cockermouth. His natural rotundity was enhanced by several extra layers of clothing and crowned by a broadbrimmed demi-bateau, and at present he was reading through a bundle of legal-looking documents tied round with pink tape, which he had produced from the small leather valise on his knees.

The fourth corner was occupied by Colonel Sir Richard Severall, Bart, late of His Majesty's Nth Dragoons, awaiting official notification of his invaliding-out from the Marquess of Wellington's army in the Peninsula. He had appeared at breakfast in the full glory of his regimentals—red coat with a liberal quantity of gold braid on the front, spotless white trousers, glossy black boots and a heavy straight sabre with the type of gold-plated hilt found on weapons presented by the Patriotic Fund—explaining apologetically that after seven years' active service, he had no civilian clothes fit to wear. The red and gold was now hidden under a voluminous ankle-length Garrick redingote, with several capes and a number of straps and buckles for controlling its ample folds. His brown eyes were almost invisible under the peak of a most uncomfortable-looking brass helmet with a black horsehair plume, but they were fixed on Miss Minster's face as he tried to recall of whom it was that she reminded him. From time to time he shifted his position and unobtrusively tried to ease the incessant ache in his right knee.

The fifth passenger was seated foursquare between Miss Minster and Mr. Tupper, bolt upright, arms folded and eyes fixed firmly on the back of the opposite seat. His presence had caused an argument when they first boarded the coach in the innyard at Kendal, for he was Sir Richard's manservant Jem, and Mr. Tupper had objected to his being allowed inside. Sir Richard had replied with a pleasant smile, and a thread of steel under his agreeable, courteous tones, that no servant of his was going to travel outside in such cold weather, for outside passengers had been known to freeze to death from time to time, or become stupefied with cold and fall off, and that there was plenty of room inside.

Mr. Tupper had countered with an irritable pronouncement that the cross-mail was supposed to carry only four inside, at which the guard, a dour Lancastrian who considered that the purpose of a mail-coach was to carry mail and deliver it on time, and that passengers were an irrelevant and frequently troublesome complication, politely informed him that the Regulations allowed for six inside if the majority of the first four made no objection. He then asked Miss Minster's opinion, which was firmly against anyone being expected to go on the roof when there was room inside. Mr. Petts replied succinctly "No," when asked if he objected, and the guard ruled Mr. Tupper outvoted, adding, "Besides, his fare's already paid."

Jem, who had remained silent throughout, little bright brown eyes darting from one speaker to another, raised his beaver to Miss Minster, revealing that his hair had been close-cropped, but was now long enough to stand up straight all over his head, which, with his snub nose and small eyes, made him look remarkably like a hedgehog. He then helped his master aboard with a heave from behind up the high step, for Sir Richard's injured leg was very stiff. His heavy sabre caught Miss Minster a sharp crack on the ankle, but she bit her lip and remained silent, thinking that the poor man had enough to contend with, getting himself, his leg and his walking-stick into the coach.

At first, Jem had seated himself between Sir Richard and Mr. Petts, but Miss Minster had suggested that it would be better if he changed sides, giving Sir Richard more room to turn sideways and stretch his stiff leg out if he wished. This suggestion was well received, Sir Richard adding, "If it won't cramp you, or Mr. Tupper, too much," with a mischievous grin at the solicitor, who snapped, "I don't know what things are coming to! In my young days, servants didn't travel inside with their betters, nor respectable young ladies travel unchaperoned in a public vehicle!'' and then obviously regretted at least the last part of his remark.

"Not every young lady is in the fortunate position of having a maid, or the means to hire a duenna!" Sir Richard had replied icily. "Miss Minster happens to be a governess travelling to take up a new situation. I think an apology is called for." He had acquired that piece of information at breakfast, before Mr. Tupper and Mr. Petts appeared.

Mr. Tupper had apologised with good grace, and Miss Minster had covered her embarrassment with a graceful and composed inclination of the head in acceptance. Conversation had then lapsed as the cross-mail set out on its journey, and no-one had spoken since.

Miss Minster had been staring unseeingly out of the window and thinking back over her long journey from Kent, and worrying over the cost of it—two pounds from Maidstone to London, six shillings for a lumpy bed in an attic room at "The Swan with Two Nicks" in the capital, and then another five pounds from London to Kendal on the Glasgow stage—the Mail would have cost twice as much—plus all the tips and meals and nights' lodgings on the way. Thank goodness there had been no delay, for this would be the last coach on the Kendal-Cockermouth route until next March, because the road ran over something called Dunmail Raise, which she had been told was usually impassable for a vehicle in winter, and so from Christmas until Spring the Mail was carried by a man on a pony. At least this part was not too expensive—only five shillings—but she must still find tips for the driver and guard, and it might be necessary to dine, and even stay the night, in Cockermouth—another half-guinea at least. It would leave her only a couple of shillings to last until her first half-year's salary was paid in June.

She sighed unconsciously and opened her reticule, seeking her new employer's letter, and read it yet again to be sure what it said about the last few miles from Cockermouth. At least it quite certainly said that a conveyance would be sent to meet her, and she would be spared the trouble of finding some way of getting to Sir Marmaduke Partridge's residence. She could not help smiling at the absurd name, but the letter was coldly formal and very brief, giving only instructions for getting to the house from London, the information that her services were required for two girls, and that her salary of twenty pounds per annum was to be paid half-yearly in arrears. There was no expression of welcome or hope that she would find the situation congenial, and it left her with a nagging doubt about the wisdom of coming so far to live in this wild part of the country among such cold-seeming strangers. However, the agency had not received any other applications for her services, so... She sighed again and shivered.

Sir Richard, who had noted both sighs and the anxiety in her grey eyes, also observed the shiver, and said peremptorily to Jem, "What did you do with the travelling-rug?"

"'Sunder your seat," Jem replied, adding "Sir," as an afterthought as he had done for the past six years.

Sir Richard leaned forward and poked about unavailingly under the bench seat with his stick, but Jem dropped to his knees in the straw and pulled out a neatly-folded parcel tied up with string, which he put beside his master before resuming his seat. "Cold enough ter mike yer turn up yer toes!" he remarked.

"It is plaguey cold, ain't it?" Sir Richard said affably to Miss Minster, untying the string and shaking out the rug, which he then spread over her, covering her from her neck to her feet. "There, tuck that round you—it'll keep the draught out."

Miss Minster made the proper polite protests, but was firmly overruled, and then snuggled gratefully under the warm rug, wrapping some of it round her feet and ankles, which had been suffering in the icy gale blowing under the door.

Now that someone had broken the silence, Mr. Tupper was emboldened to look over his spectacles at Sir Richard and enquire with tentatively friendly intent, "I see you walk with a stick, sir. I deduce that you may be on sick leave from the Peninsula?"

"I'm awaiting my discharge," Sir Richard replied. "A dragoon that's lame in the off-side hind ain't much use to the Beau—the Marquess of Wellington," he added as his audience looked blank at the nickname.

"I suppose it would be a little difficult," Mr. Tupper observed.

"Difficult? You may well say so! Mounting a horse, to start with—can't start searching round for a mounting-block with the Beau looking down his beak and awaiting your *earliest* convenience!"

"Not ter mention Johnny Crapoh chuckin' 'eavy metal at yer!" Jem added sepulchrally. Sir Richard quelled him with a severe look.

"How did you come to be injured?" Mr. Tupper asked with apparent interest.

Sir Richard was disinclined to reply at first, then changed his mind and said off-handedly, "Damn' silly business. We were crossing the Zadora early last summer—nothing much going on, hardly a Frenchy in sight. I was sitting m'horse on the north bank, watching m'men safely across, when some zealous idiot—on our *own* side, would you believe?—opened up with a couple of nine-pounder popguns. I saw one of the balls hit a rock near me, and watched a splinter fly off and hit me in the side of the leg—lifted m'knee-cap straight off! Very aggravating." He caught sight of Miss Minster's shocked expression and added, "Sorry—not a suitable subject for a lady's ears—do apologise!"

"Not at all. It must have been terribly painful. Is it healing well?" she asked, recovering her normal self-possession.

"As there was nothing much going on, the butchers had time to see to it properly instead of just—er—amputating. It's healed quite well, but it's left the knee stiff and unreliable."

"It'll improve in time. You 'as to be patient," Jem encouraged him, clearly not by any means for the first time.

"Mum your dubber," Sir Richard said equably. "You're a damn' sight too talkative. Remind me to hand you over to the first High Tobyman we meet instead of m'watch!"

"Ere!" Jem exclaimed in alarm. "Don't mike jokes abaht the 'Igh Toby! That ain't a subjick for joking *a tall*!"

"No, indeed!" Mr. Tupper added reprovingly. "Highway robbery is not a subject for humour!"

Mr. Petts opened his eyes, darted a quick look round his companions, and then said to Mr. Tupper, "Do you get much drag-laying round 'ere?"

"Not a great deal," the solicitor replied, "although I must admit that we are somewhat troubled by a small band of desperadoes at present. Two or three, working together. Their leader calls himself 'Black Beelzebub'."

"Do they work the cross-mail?" Mr. Petts asked.

"Oh no! They never hold up the Mail! That is a very serious offence!" Mr. Tupper sounded shocked.

"Ighway robbery's ripe for a Newgate 'ornpipe anyway!" Mr. Petts said scornfully. "What's this Beelzebub fellow like?"

"Well, he wears a mask, of course—they all do—and he is said to be tall, rather thin, but broad-shouldered, and sounds like a Southerner," Mr. Tupper replied. "The magistrates are considering calling in a thief-taker, I understand." He was obviously chagrined at having given the impression that he did not know that any kind of highway robbery was a hanging offence.

Mr. Petts grunted and closed his eyes again, apparently losing interest in the subject.

"Mails get drag-layed quite orfen," Jem volunteered. "I was reading at the Post Orfice that one gets done ev'ry night. Larst Jan'ry the guard on one going through Whitechapel stood up ter blow 'is yard o' tin and some willian stole all the packets outer the dickey afore 'e could sit dahn agen!"

Sir Richard extended his good leg and gently kicked his servant on the ankle, caught his eyes, and shook his head. Jem at once turned to Miss Minster and said comfortingly, "Don't yer worrit none, Miss! Me and the Colonel 'll look arter yer if this Black Beezlebub shows up!"

Miss Minster replied, "Thank you," and then, suddenly catching a glimpse of wind-ruffled grey water through the opposite window, exclaimed, "Oh! Is that Lake Windermere?"

Mr. Tupper looked at it carefully and admitted that her surmise was correct. "Although it is tautological to call it *Lake* Windermere," he added, "For Windermere means 'the winding lake'. Because it—er—winds," he clarified. "It is the largest lake in England." Having instructed the uninformed, he returned to his legal papers without giving the lake a second glance, and Sir Richard, under cover of the creaking and rumbling of the coach, murmured just loud enough for Miss Minster to hear:

> "A primrose by a river's brim,
> A yellow primrose was to him,
> And it was nothing more."

at which she could not forbear to smile. This brought about an almost startling transformation in her appearance, for it lit her eyes and revealed a very pretty dimple beside her mouth, and a row of even pearly teeth. Sir Richard, who had thought her a subdued and rather dowdy young lady before, was pleasantly surprised.

"You are well-acquainted with the works of Mr. Wordsworth?" she enquired.

"Oh, m'sister's always quoting the fellow. She married into an estate at Bridekirk, north of Cockermouth, and lives here half the year now. I'm on m'way there for Christmas."

"You don't live hereabouts then?" Miss Minster asked, feeling a little disappointed, as Sir Richard had seemed an approachable person who might possibly be asked for a little information about her new employer.

"No. I've an estate in Hampshire, and a London house, of course, but they've both been shut up for six or seven years and can't be made ready in time. I'd not care to live here, for all it's wild and romantic, if you like that kind of thing. I prefer good arable and a neat bit of coppice m'self."

"Yes." Miss Minster had been trying to avoid thinking about the unfavourable impression the grey fells, now looming immediately ahead, had made on her spirits. "I believe Mr. Wordsworth lives hereabouts?" she asked, directing her question to Mr. Tupper.

He looked up, one finger keeping his place on the page he was reading. "Indeed," he replied. "At Rydal Mount. You won't see it from the road, but if I remember, I'll point out the cottage in which he used to live as we pass. You admire his work?"

"Some of it," Miss Minster replied cautiously. "At his best, I think he is very fine, but sometimes he seems..." As she hesitated, Sir Richard supplied "Damn' pedestrian," which conveyed the meaning she sought, if it was not expressed in terms she might employ.

"Well, I always told him that poetry's all very well for a pastime," Mr. Tupper pontificated. "But hardly a means of earning a good living! 'William' I used to say to him, 'William, you'd do better to work hard at University, obtain a First, and then settle to a proper profession, and leave your verse to your spare time,' but I wasted my breath, of course! He played the fool when he should have been studying, only obtained a pass degree, and then went gallyvanting abroad, picking up these odd French ideas..." He pronounced "French" as if it were some unpleasant disease, and tailed off into a number of exasperated shakes of the head.

"You are acquainted with Mr. Wordsworth?" Miss Minster was suitably impressed.

"Oh, yes! I was junior to a close friend of his father, who was agent to Sir James Lowther, you know—who is Earl of Lonsdale now. Old Mr. Wordsworth died when William was still a child, and my master was one of the boy's trustees. I suppose he'd done quite well at his writing, but it doesn't provide his real income—he derives that from being the local agent for stamps."

"Stamps?" enquired Miss Minster blankly.

"For legal documents—contracts, and so forth. Stamp duty," Mr. Tupper enlarged, and then suddenly turned to

Sir Richard and observed, "You must find a public mail-coach uncomfortable, sir? One never knows with whom one will be expected to associate." He could not resist a discreetly disparaging glance at Jem. "I apprehend that you keep no carriage in England if you have been so long abroad."

"I bought a spanking new 'chaise in London," Sir Richard replied, "but the damn' thing contracted a cracked felloe, or some such ailment, just short of Kendal. I've left Henry Coachman with it, for the nearest wheelwright lives in Kirkby Lonsdale, and wouldn't come out today, tomorrow being Christmas Eve. Henry'll bring it on to m'sister's when it's repaired."

Mr. Tupper nodded his understanding and sympathy, glanced out of the window again, and then packed his papers away inside his valise with, "We stop in a few minutes."

Even as he spoke, the guard played a lively turn on his horn, and a minute or two later, the coach slowed and came to rest outside a small inn. The guard was down almost before it stopped, flung open the offside door, and announced, "Ten minutes, if you please, Madam and Sirs!" before hurrying into the inn with his timeclock and pouch of bye-mail. Miss Minster noticed that he had overlaid his sharp North-country speech with a veneer of careful correctness, presumably to make himself comprehensible to travelling Southerners.

Sir Richard sent Jem ahead with a commanding, "Five hot grogs at the double!" and then descended himself, landing awkwardly on his right leg, which was cramped with cold and long-sitting. It gave way, but he saved himself with his stick and uttered an angry, "Blast it!"

Miss Minster had not heard the expression before, and as he turned to hand her down, he encountered her startled expression and added apologetically. "I'm sorry—the damn' thing annoys me!" which did not much help matters.

Mr. Petts and Mr. Tupper had got down on their own side, and Miss Minster followed them into the inn, glancing up at the sky on her way. A thick pall of yellowish cloud now covered it, hanging low on the slopes of the nearest fells, and a few feathery white crystals brushed her upturned face. Sir Richard paused for a moment to invite the driver to join him for some refreshment, but he replied, "N'thankee, sir. Ah never takes strong drink whiles Ah'm on root."

The inn parlour was small and rather dark, but a good log fire crackled in the hearth, and Miss Minster went to it thankfully, chafing her hands and extending first one foot and then the other towards the heat. A waiter trotted in with a tray of steaming rummers, and Sir Richard said, "My stand, gentlemen!" at which Mr. Petts and Mr. Tupper ceased to ferret for money in their many layers of clothing and thanked him very much. He took two glasses and carried one of them to Miss Minster, sipping the other as he went. He had taken off his helmet and hung it by its chinstrap on his arm, revealing crisp brown hair brushed into a curly Brutus.

"This will warm you," he said.

"Oh!" exclaimed Miss Minster. "I didn't—I mean, I was not going to have anything. Thank you—you're very kind," as he put the rummer into her gloved hands, where it at once sent a warm glow coursing through her fingers. She added a little nervous smile, at which his brown eyes twinkled and he raised his own glass in a silent toast.

The steaming liquid was light brown in colour, and Miss Minster thought it was lemon tea, so she took quite a mouthful, then choked a little as it seared its way down her throat and dropped like liquid fire into her stomach. "Oh, what is it?" she exclaimed.

"Grog. Brandy and water with a little sugar and spice."

"I've never taken brandy before," she said dubiously.

"It's quite safe—half of it's water—but it will put some warmth into you. It's a good drink for cold weather—m'sister always serves it to guests in the winter," Sir Richard told her encouragingly.

Miss Minster sipped it cautiously, and as it did not blow her head off nor cause her to fall on the floor in a drunken stupor, she decided it was harmless and drank it gratefully. Jem, standing in the doorway but not actually entering the parlour, despite his entitlement to do so as the holder of an inside ticket, allowed what could only be described as a smirk to appear on his face, which earned him a cold and unencouraging glare from his master. He sobered at once and withdrew with his grog to the front door, where he could watch the new team being put to.

Presently, the guard sounded the Crack of Doom on his horn, and the passengers hurried to resume their places. The coachman walked round his team, appeared to have a short argument with one of the ostlers, eventually nodded, heaved himself on to his box, gathered his ribbons, and shouted "Reet away!" which was echoed by the guard. The ostlers whipped off the horseblankets, the guard blew another blast, and they were off again.

"I wonder what the village is called?" Miss Minster mused aloud as they clattered over a stone bridge and past a few cottages.

"Troutbeck Bridge," Mr. Tupper was already back among his papers, and Mr. Petts apparently sound asleep.

"Dragsman didn't like the orf-side wheeler," Jem informed his master. "Can't say I do, neether. Looks a rum cuss ter me."

"Oh? Why's that?"

"Well, 'e kicked 'is ostler, bucked at the trices, bit 'is leader, and leered 'orribly!"

"Sounds an unfriendly brute. He's a she, by the way. Ten years in the Heavy Cavalry, and you can't tell a mare from a gelding? Really, Jem!"

"All 'orses is 'es ter me," Jem replied lugubriously, folded his arms and resumed his contemplation of the opposite seat.

There was a silence for a while, apart from the noise of the coach and the pounding of the team's hooves. Miss Minster stared blankly out at the heights which blocked the view northwards and rose halfway up the sky. They looked bleak and forbidding. The valley-side which rose from the side of the road was pleasantly wooded and comfortingly familiar in appearance to one reared in the Weald of Kent, but those bare mountains were hostile and sinister, and her spirits sank at the thought of spending the next ten years or so of her life among them.

There was no other course open to her, however. Her comparative youth and lack of experience would have deterred many families from employing her, and the one or two interviews she had been granted had unaccountably resulted in polite refusals, which had upset her at first, until one fond mamma and prospective employer of a governess had explained the reason by saying apologetically, "I think you'd be very good for dearest Sophia, but unfortunately, I have two susceptible sons in their early twenties, and you're far too pretty, my dear!"

Miss Minster had never considered herself pretty, and, in fact, she was not. Her features were fashioned in a classical mode, and in repose she looked coolly detached and unapproachable, but when she was smiling, or animated in conversation, she had some claim to be thought a Beauty. Unfortunately, she never happened to be look-ing in a mirror at those times, and so remained unaware of the fact.

The coach gave a sudden curious lurch, as if it had hic-coughed, and then continued as comparatively smoothly as before.

"That were the orf-side wheeler. Tole yer so, didn' I?" Jem said in satisfied tones. "''E jinked. Don' like the snow, I shouldn't wonder!"

"Who does?" Sir Richard enquired bitterly.

Miss Minster, jogged out of her reverie by this ex-change, realised that while she had been staring at it without seeing it, the landscape had been undergoing a transformation, and was already partially obscured by a fall of large snowflakes. The roadside verges were cov-ered, and clumps were forming among the twigs of the bare trees.

"It is really becoming quite heavy!" Mr. Tupper said, inspecting it over his spectacles. "Yes, I think I may safely say it is a heavy fall."

Presently, the coach clattered into Ambleside and made a brief stop while the guard delivered another pouch of mail. As he returned to the coach, Mr. Tupper pulled down the window and put his head out, keeping a firm grip on his demi-bateau. "Guard! I say, guard!" he called.

"Yes, what is it, sir?" the guard asked, his voice sounding apprehensive. He lived in constant anxiety that something might happen to delay the coach so that the mail actually arrived late and earned him a reprimand from the Postmaster-General.

"Is it wise to proceed?" Mr. Tupper enquired.

"Ah has to go on," replied the guard, sounding both complacent and aggrieved, as if he considered that he was safe from the problems of having to make a decision, but also resented his consequent lack of freedom.

"Yes, yes, of course—the mail must be delivered!" Mr. Tupper cried testily. "I meant for a passenger!"

"You must please yourself about that," the guard replied. "It's not my place to advise t'gentry. This coach will go on to Cockermouth, given we can get over t'Raise, and Ah don't see why we shouldn't, for it's not drifting yet."

Mr. Tupper withdrew his head and closed the window, receiving a frosty glare from Mr. Petts, who was brushing his coat to get rid of the flakes which had blown in on him, and the coach started moving again.

"I'd not care to be snowed up in a coach for Christmas," Mr. Tupper told the company. "However, the guard seems confident that it will not come to that. I trust he may be right! I really would not advise anyone to travel in this part of the world in winter! Oh, if only I could have finished my business in Kendal a day earlier!"

"Winter," said Jem reflectively. "Gawd! 'Ow I 'ates winter! It reminds me of Corunna!"

"Yes," said Sir Richard briefly.

"Were—were you in the Retreat?" Miss Minster enquired hesitantly, looking at Sir Richard with wide-eyed respect.

"We both were."

"It must have been terrible!" she offered tentatively, conscious that it had been far worse than anything she could imagine.

"Indescribable," Sir Richard gave her a bleak smile to soften any idea that he was snubbing her. "So I shan't bore you by attempting a description. Mr. Tupper, where do we change cattle again?"

"At Grasmere Town Head," the solicitor replied, "before the Raise. We may take on an extra beast if the driver considers it desirable."

"A steamer," Sir Richard supplied the proper term.

"Ah yes, a steamer indeed," Mr. Tupper agreed, and having been distracted from his papers, obligingly glanced out of the window and observed, "Rydal Water."

Miss Minster leaned forward, turning her head in order to see it past the demi-bateau, and was very disconcerted when Sir Richard did the same, and she suddenly found herself cheek by jowl with him. Their eyes met, and some little gleam in Sir Richard's made her sit back in her seat with a jerk, feeling an unaccustomed flutter in her throat and a warm flush in her cheeks. Neither of them saw the lake.

"Really!" Miss Minster told herself. "Set in a fluster by a handsome soldier, like a silly chit of a girl! Whatever next!" and sternly repressed the thought that he *was* handsome. Unfortunately, she inadvertently looked at him, and found that he was watching her and smiling, and concluded that he must have seen her colour rise, and was amused about it. She kept her attention on the whirl of snowflakes outside her window, and when, after another fifteen minutes or so, Mr. Tupper said "Grasmere," she glanced at Sir Richard, who made a little gesture to convey that she might lean forward with impunity. She did so, and caught a fleeting glimpse of yellow reedbeds and an area of grey water.

Soon after, the road turned quite sharply to pass between two hills, and the resultant lurch of the coach caused Mr. Tupper to look up again, and he remembered to say, "Ah, there is Townend Cottage, the Wordsworths' former home!"

Miss Minster looked to his side of the coach, saw that he was pointing to her side, and turned back just in time to catch sight of the whitewashed cottage set among trees behind a low stone wall.

"It looks remarkably poky!" Sir Richard observed. "With a poet, his wife and sister, and three or four children, not to mention all the other poets who visit him, all crowded into that little place—one wonders how he found space and peace enough to write at all!"

"That is why he moved to Rydal Mount!" Mr. Tupper said drily as the coach slowed to negotiate the narrow street and many corners of Grasmere village.

After that, the road began to climb more steeply, and the white-covered fells seemed to reach out to crowd about the coach. Miss Minster looked up at their steep sides and thought what a wild, bleak, unwelcoming appearance they had. It was quite frightening to think of living among them for any length of time, and although they might be very grand, romantic and beautiful in summer, the winter here must start earlier and go on for longer than in the softer country in the south. It would be lonely, and cold in more than a physical sense. She shivered, feeling bitterly homesick for Kent, for all she had lost.

"We almost need a steamer for this hill," Sir Richard observed. "It's very hard on the cattle, so near the end of a stage."

A few minutes later, they stopped outside the Town Head inn, the team blowing and hanging their heads under a small steam-cloud of their own making.

"Forty minutes, if you please!" the guard announced, opening the offside door. "Luncheon will be served immediately."

"That's early!" Sir Richard observed as he descended. "It's barely half-past eleven!"

"There's no good inn after this until Keswick," the guard explained. "And t'driver needs to be rested and fresh to tackle t'Raise."

"What is the Raise?" Miss Minster asked as Sir Richard handed her down. The guard pointed in reply, and she looked to the left and saw that beyond the tollgate the road continued to rise steeply, and then to wind from side to side, zig-zag fashion, both rising and receding between two monstrous hills until it was swallowed up in the narrow pass. Even as she looked, the falling snow thickened and came down like a curtain, blotting out the upper part of the Raise.

"It's not as bad as it looks," the guard said reassuringly, seeing her apprehensive expression.

"I should hope not!" Sir Richard exclaimed, and Miss Minster, realising that he was still holding her hand, gently freed herself and hurried across the crisp snow to the inn.

As she reached the door, someone cried out in alarm behind her, and turning to see what it was, she was just in time to witness the offside wheeler celebrate the end of her stage by kicking an ostler for the second time in one day, and then, just as Jem had described earlier, leering in a truly horrible fashion, showing a large number of big yellow teeth.

CHAPTER TWO

A DOLEFUL LOOKING waiter with a large red nose and bleary eyes was passing through the hallway. He indicated to Miss Minster the whereabouts of a small retiring-room where she could remove her cloak and bonnet and wash her face and hands in the warm water standing ready in a can, and then tidy her hair, which was drawn back rather severely from her face, twisted into a coil, and pinned high on the back of her head. Then, feeling refreshed, she went to the parlour to warm herself at the fire.

She found the room empty, but a second door stood half open, and through it she could see a dining-room, where Mr. Tupper could be heard informing Mr. Petts that he really would not advise something or other. Miss Minster smiled a little, laid her cloak and bonnet on a high-backed oak settle, and held out her hands to the logs burning in the big fireplace. She was sorely tempted to take luncheon, for the effects of the grog at Troutbeck Bridge had worn off long ago and she felt thoroughly chilled, wretched and hungry.

"Ah, there you are!" exclaimed Sir Richard, appearing in the dining-room doorway. "Ain't you coming in to luncheon?"

"No, thank you. I—I'm not hungry," she replied, not sounding as careless about it as she would have wished.

"But you must be—you can't travel all day in this bitter weather with nothing inside you!"

"I took breakfast..."

"Two pieces of toast and a dish of tea!" Sir Richard said scornfully. "My dear girl! A mouse couldn't survive on that!"

"I am not your dear girl, and I do not wish to take luncheon!" Miss Minster kept her face turned towards the fire and tried to sound cold and haughty, but only succeeded in sounding close to tears, which she was.

Sir Richard pushed the door to behind him and entered the room far enough to stand close beside her, and peered at her profile. "What's to do, m'dear?" he asked quietly. "Didn't your new employer send enough blunt for your journey?"

"He didn't send any," she replied. "A governess is expected to pay her own travelling expenses."

"That's the trouble, then? You ain't got the necessary for luncheon?"

She did not answer, but her silence was sufficient reply.

"I'd be happy to lend you a few guineas..." he suggested tentatively.

"You're very kind, but it would be most improper, and I couldn't repay it for months..." She sounded and felt very desolate.

"I take it a governess is actually *paid* for her services?"

"Oh yes! Half-yearly. I shall receive ten pounds in June." She made a little movement with her hands as if to express her fatalistic acceptance of the position, and it touched a chord in Sir Richard's memory, recalling someone else who had that same habit.

"Are you by any chance Sir John Minster's daughter?" he asked.

She turned her head to stare at him, her heart giving a sudden lurch of shock which reflected in her expressive grey eyes, and she looked as if he had struck her.

"What if I am?" she asked in a cold, hostile tone, and turned her back on him.

Puzzled by her reaction, Sir Richard said mildly, "It's just that the way you moved your hands then reminded me of him. I knew him quite well some years ago. In fact, when I first went into Society, he was very kind to me—helped me out of a scrape."

Miss Minster's stiffly-held shoulders seemed to relax a little, and she half-turned her head towards him, as if to hear him better.

"I'd bought a mare at Tatt's—a good, sound grey—but she cost me more than I expected, and I'd overdrawn my allowance—daren't tell m'father, who was deuced strict in such matters. Your father lent me the necessary until next quarter-day."

There was a silence for a moment, and Miss Minster turned a little more towards him, relaxing still further, so he ventured, "He is your father?"

"He was."

"He's dead then? I'm sorry—I didn't know."

She faced him fully and looked up at him, her eyes filled with tears.

"He died four years ago. By his own hand."

Sir Richard looked at her with an expression of shocked concern on his pleasant features.

"Oh, Lord! I *am* sorry!" He hesitated, looking as if he might be about to ask why, but instead he went on, "I've committed a *faux pas*, but I assure you it was in ignorance! Now look, you must let me buy you luncheon, or I'll be afflicted with strong feelings of guilt!''

Miss Minster had endured many cold looks and withdrawals from former friends and acquaintances when they had heard of her father's suicide, and a few expressions of sympathy, spoken in hushed voices as though to the innocent victim of a thoughtless, criminal action, but Sir Richard's reaction was quite novel in her experience. His expressions of sympathy and apology were undoubtedly genuine and, indeed, heartfelt, for all their brevity, but he did not dwell on them almost gloatingly, as some people would have done. He continued in a dramatic fashion, worthy of Mr. Kemble at his worst, ''I shall Worry myself Sick about you all afternoon, travelling in this Arctic Waste on an empty stomach! I shall probably Fling myself About in a Distressed and Agitated Fashion, and I might even Groan! Heartrendingly!''

Blinking away the tears which had blurred her vision, Miss Minster, disconcerted, looked at him in a puzzled, searching manner, at which he put his head on one side and said coaxingly, ''Please come and eat—you'll find it much less embarrassing than the extravagant behaviour caused by my tormented conscience, which would probably go on all the way to Cockermouth!''

She made no reply at first, but allowed him to take her hand and lead her towards the dining-room. As he opened the door and stood aside for her to pass through, she said, ''Thank you,'' in a quiet, subdued voice.

''My pleasure,'' he replied, equally quietly, with his engaging smile, but she kept her eyes down as she went into the room, and did not see it.

Mr. Petts and Mr. Tupper were already seated on opposite sides of the square table. They stood up at Miss Minster's entrance, Mr. Petts in a somewhat perfunctory fashion and only half-rising. She and Sir Richard took the remaining places, and the doleful waiter came in at that moment with a steaming tureen, which he set before Sir Richard with a professional instinct for selecting the person of highest social rank present, and the curious incantation, "Grey-pez keal!"

It proved to be a thick broth made with dried peas, hot and very sustaining. It was followed by a delicious leg of roast mutton, served with rowan jelly, boiled cabbage and roast potatoes. Sir Richard carved and helped Miss Minster to the Pope's eye, an attention which she found much in contrast to the usual fashion in which a governess was served with meals—alone in a cold schoolroom, brought by an ungracious housemaid, half-cold and made up from left-overs from the family table.

Mr. Tupper said that he thought he might safely say that the mutton was as fine as any he had tasted, and Sir Richard replied that the sheep of Cumberland and Westmoreland were justly famed for their excellent meat, which Mr. Tupper clearly took as a compliment to his native heath, and therefore to himself. Mr. Petts ate in silence, but passed up his plate for a second helping with a dour, "Wery passable bit of woolly-bird, that!"

Miss Minster had not previously heard that term for a sheep and her imagination readily conjured up a flock of large birds with sheep's heads and wool for feathers, hopping about on the fellsides, a picture which considerably restored her spirits and led her to accept a second serving herself and tackle it with good appetite.

The light meal was completed by a large gooseberry pie, and a platter of crusty new bread and crumbly white cheese, and a choice of ale or tea. The gentlemen chose the former, leaving Miss Minster the whole pot of tea for herself, and she was glad to take two cups.

Punctual to the exact forty minutes, the guard appeared in the dining-room doorway with his posthorn in his hand, and Sir Richard exclaimed, "I bet you'll not sound that in here! You'll rouse the whole place and make us fear the Scots have invaded!"

The guard replied unsmilingly, "Ah'm about to sound *outside*, for t'tollkeeper. T'cattle are to, Madam and Sirs, and won't improve with waiting in t'cold."

The passengers obediently collected their belongings and donned their respective coats, cloaks and headgear. The waiter appeared and collected his dues from Mr. Tupper and Mr. Petts. As he approached Sir Richard and Miss Minster, she opened her reticule to take out her purse, but Sir Richard firmly closed it again with one hand while he paid the waiter for both with the other, and replied to her whispered thanks with a smile.

In the hallway, they found Mr. Tupper exchanging a hearty handshake with a slightly-built middle-aged man who had apparently just come in, and they heard him exclaim, "My dear William! How good to see you looking so well! And how is Mrs. Wordsworth, and Miss Dorothy? Well, I trust? And the children?"

Miss Minster and Sir Richard exchanged a look of surmise, and the next moment Mr. Tupper was begging leave to make known his old friend Mr. Wordsworth to them both.

Miss Minster looked at the poet with some awe as she acknowledged the introduction with a suitable inclination in reply to his bow. He looked fairly ordinary, with receding hair, bushy eyebrows and the weatherbeaten complexion of a man much out of doors, but his deep-set eyes, she fancied, had an unusual brilliance, and his strongly curving, long nose gave his features an interesting touch of character. She said a few words of admiration for his work and appreciation of the honour of meeting him, at which he looked modestly down his nose and replied in what she could only describe as an educated North country accent.

Sir Richard also expressed pleasure at meeting his sister's favourite poet, and then the guard sounded an impatient fanfare in the forecourt, and the passengers had to hurry out to the coach, where the guard informed them that it would be necessary for them to walk up the Raise, as the steamer had gone lame. "T'lady and t'Military Gentleman may ride if they wish," he added graciously.

Mr. Tupper tut-tutted in an irritable fashion, and Sir Richard said apologetically that he was afraid he could not possibly walk so far, even if it were not snowing, or else he would have been happy to offer Mr. Tupper his place, at which the solicitor assured him that it was of no consequence, and far from the first time that he had walked up the Raise.

Sir Richard handed Miss Minster into the coach, heaved himself up the high step, and took his place opposite her, but nearer the middle of the vehicle than before, to help balance it. He passed her the travelling rug, and remarked, looking out the window, "It's snowing more heavily than ever, and the flakes are smaller. I believe that's a bad sign."

"Yes," she replied. "This seems a very harsh, wild country."

"What possessed you to accept a situation so far north?" he asked. "Your home is—was—in Kent, I believe?"

"Yes, and so was my last position, in Maidstone. After—after my father died, my own old governess helped me to get it, for a friend of hers had been forced to retire through ill-health. I was there until November, but now my charge has come out, and I had to apply to an agency for another place. I was granted two or three interviews, but I was thought too young and inexperienced, and this was the only offer of employment that I received. I could not afford to wait any longer in hopes of something further south.''

"No, I suppose not. What is the name of your new employers? M'sister may know them."

"Sir Marmaduke Partridge," Miss Minster again could not help but smile at the name, and Sir Richard gave a crow of laughter. "Poor devil!" he commented.

When he had recovered, he looked as if he was seeking a way of proceeding to a more difficult topic, and Miss Minster turned away to look out of the window, hoping he would not do so. The team had already hauled the coach up the first of the traverses, and the inn at Town Head was barely visible through the falling snow, which completely obscured the valley below. Sir Richard apparently realised that she was trying to avoid further personal conversation, and there was silence for some time.

At the next turn in the road, there was a flurry of agitation, the coachman shouting to the guard and cracking his long whip, and the coach lurched alarmingly. Sir Richard took off his helmet, pulled down the window, and put his head out, then reported to Miss Minster that the nearside leader had slipped and almost come down, and had now become entangled in his own traces, but Jem was helping the guard to sort things out.

"He's remarkably good with horses, despite his claim that he doesn't like them, or they him!"

"I suppose he served under you in the Army?" she replied.

"Yes. We saved each other's lives a few times on the way to Corunna, and since, and he asked to be my servant when we returned to Portugal with Sir Arthur—the Marquess, as he is now. When I was discharged unfit from the hospital, he wanted to remain with me, so I bought him out. He's a good servant, apart from his unfortunate lack of oral discretion, which is little short of disastrous! I'm forever apologising for his language, or his outrageous comments!''

"But you wouldn't be without him."

Sir Richard closed the window and smiled at her as he resumed his seat. He really had a very attractive smile. It made his mouth look a little lop-sided, and crinkled the skin about his eyes, which twinkled in a very lively fashion. In fact, he was an attractive man altogether, being tall and well-proportioned. His hair, ruffled by the wind outside and sprinkled with a few snowflakes, curled stubbornly, despite any amount of brushing and smoothing. Miss Minster judged him to be about thirty at the most, despite his high military rank, but she knew that he had probably attained that by purchase.

"The other two are plodding along behind," he remarked. "Mr. Tupper seems to be managing very well, and Mr. Petts strides along as if he has been walking the fells all his life."

"I'd have thought he would be more at home in Cheapside," Miss Minster replied. "He's a very silent man."

"Something of a mystery."

"Yes. He seems quite out of place in this part of the world—more like a shopkeeper, I think, but he is very well equipped for winter travel, and his coat and hat are far from new."

"He seems to be a seasoned traveller," Sir Richard said encouragingly.

"I wondered if he might be something to do with the coach company, or the Post Office—I suppose they have inspectors of some sort? But he hasn't so much as glanced at the horses or the stables, and he doesn't look at his watch at all, to check the timekeeping."

"You're very observant!" Sir Richard sounded approving. "Have you noticed the one thing which did rouse him out of his pretence of being asleep, if only for a few minutes?"

"The highwayman."

"Yes, and the highwayman is said to be tall, thin, but broadshouldered, and sounds like a Southerner, which might well describe Mr. Petts himself!"

"You don't think . . . ?" Miss Minster began apprehensively.

Sir Richard looked at her too-pale, too-serious face and those very fine eyes which were far too often clouded with anxiety or unhappiness, and felt a strong desire to kick someone, without being any too sure whom, or why.

"Well, if he is, he can hardly hold us up while he's travelling in the same coach!" he pointed out with comforting common sense.

"That would present certain problems," she admitted, smiling enough to show that pretty dimple again. Sir Richard contemplated her face in a frankly admiring manner, which brought a faint flush to her cheeks and made her turn her attention to the outside world again, or at least, the little which could be seen in the way of swirling snowflakes, dark outcrops of rock and an unpleasantly thick blanket of pristine whiteness.

With both passengers silent, the wind could be heard soughing in the pass, and, from time to time, Jem's voice uplifted in various horsey objurgations designed to encourage the toiling cattle. A steady, rather monotonous background noise appeared to be Mr. Tupper imparting slightly breathless enlightenment of some kind to Mr. Petts, who made no audible reply.

"What shall you do if you find life at the Partridges' disagreeable?" Sir Richard asked suddenly.

"I must hope it may not be," she replied, "For I've nowhere else to go, and only a few shillings in my purse until June. Even then, I could not seek another post, for the agency fees and the cost of travelling south again would take more than I shall receive, and leave me with nothing to live on while I find a new place."

"I suppose your family estate was entailed in the heir male," Sir Richard said tentatively. "Your brother, perhaps?"

"It was not entailed, and I was an only child," she replied in a crisp tone which was perfectly courteous, but still made it quite clear that she did not wish to discuss the matter. He took the hint and talked of indifferent subjects in an entertaining manner until the coach toiled up the last of the very steep loops in the road and stopped to allow the walking passengers to climb aboard, Mr. Petts first, after shaking himself like a large dog to free himself from the snow plastered on his coat and hat. Mr. Tupper flapped his hands ineffectually, and Jem obligingly gave him a few hearty thumps to clear the accumulations from his shoulders, whipped his hat off and tapped it smartly against the coach, and then replaced it on his head, before serving himself in the same way. Miss Minster and Sir Richard moved back to their respective corners, the latter enquiring if the others were very cold.

"Apart from the extremities, I am quite comfortable," Mr. Tupper replied. "A fairly brisk walk, even in this cold, does certainly stir up the circulation, and I should think it is quite healthy, in moderation." Mr. Petts replied, "Warm enough, thankee."

"Are you all right Jem?" Sir Richard enquired.

"Quite 'ot," that worthy answered. "''Eaving and shoving them 'orses makes yer as warm as..." He stopped and pondered, obviously searching his vocabulary for a suitable simile. Sir Richard visibly winced in anticipation of something infelicitous, and looked relieved when nothing worse than "toast" finally emerged a little lamely. He was immediately put to the blush, however, as Jem added cheerfully that he was "in a fair old muck sweat!"

The coach started to move again after the horses had been allowed to catch their breath, and went on quite slowly, as the road still ran uphill, and Mr. Tupper embarked on the recounting of a folktale about the name of the Raise. Dunmail had apparently been a warrior who fought a battle in the pass in the mists of antiquity, or of Mr. Tupper's defective memory, for he had not the least idea when, or who was involved, referring vaguely to the Vikings or the Normans, or perhaps the Scots, in a very unclear fashion. He said that there was a great cairn of stones near the top to commemorate the dead, or possibly the victors, in the battle, but when the coach passed the spot, or where it might have been if it was not elsewhere, the snow had drifted so much that nothing could be seen, and the story tailed off in an indeterminate fashion.

Once the highest point had been reached, the vehicle picked up speed as the team broke in the usual trot, and Mr. Tupper abandoned his dubious history and said with satisfaction that it was all downhill or on the level now to the next stage-point at Thirlspot, and there would only be a comparatively short uphill stretch after that before Keswick.

"And after Keswick?" Sir Richard enquired.

"Well, yes, there is the Whinlatter Pass, but it is not nearly so bad as Dunmail Raise, and, in any case, it runs from East to West, so it is protected from the north wind, and does not become too deep with snow."

"It seems to me that this road will shortly become impassable," Sir Richard observed.

"Yus. The guard said we was lucky the snow didn't start an hour earlier, or we'd not 'ave got up the Raise," Jem volunteered.

Miss Minster leaned against the side of the coach and looked out of the window again, not because she really wished to, but the scene outside seemed to attract her back to its contemplation by some kind of mesmerism. The white fellside rose steeply from the roadside and was now so high that she could not make out the top. The coach seemed to be moving quite fast now, and she assumed that the coachman had sprung his team to win clear of the higher ground before the wheels began to be bogged down in the snow.

She looked across at the far window, and thought the fellside there seemed to be less near to the road, and deduced, correctly, that there was probably a stream running alongside the road. "A beck," she thought, recalling the local name from a book she had read about the Lakes.

At that moment, the coach seemed to swing sharply to the left and gave a tremendous lurch, and then slowed abruptly, tilted forward and sideways and proceeded by a series of violent jolts which threw the passengers about alarmingly. Miss Minster, taken unawares, was flung forward and landed heavily on top of Sir Richard, who gave a grunt of surprise and with great presence of mind, seized her in both arms and clamped her to his chest until such time as things should sort themselves out.

Jem and Mr. Tupper were also projected from their places. Jem managed to twist round in flight and landed more or less sitting on the opposite seat, but the solicitor crashed on to Mr. Petts, who pushed him off with an angry, "'Ere, mind what you're doing!"

After several more violent lurches, the coach came to a standstill and canted slowly over to the offside until it was almost on its side. As it began this final movement, there was a wild shout of alarm from the driver, and the guard was heard to address his Maker in extremely agitated tones.

Then there was silence.

"We appear to have come off the road," Sir Richard remarked conversationally, after a lengthy pause. "Is anyone hurt?"

There was no answer at first, and then Mr. Petts said rather acidly that he would be better able to count his broken arms and legs if Mr. Tupper would 'ave the goodness to get orf his lap'. Jem said in a concerned tone that his beaver hat had taken a nasty knock, and Miss Minster murmured discreetly into Sir Richard's ear that she was finding it difficult to breathe. He was about to enquire further into this, fearing that she might have broken some ribs, when he realised what she meant and hastily slackened his tight embrace.

Mr. Tupper now complained indignantly that his papers were scattered all over the place, and that the coach company was very much at fault in not carrying out its undertaking to deliver both passengers and mail safely at their destination.

"Barring Acts of God," Sir Richard pointed out. "Was that the driver who gave the blood-curdling shriek?"

"I reckon 'e was flung orf 'is box," Jem replied. "Bound ter be, 'cos 'e ain't got nuffing to 'ang on to, like wot you 'as, sir!"

Sir Richard, who was still diligently "'anging on" to Miss Minster, although no longer crushing her quite so fiercely, instructed him to hold his peace and hoped that the driver had not been injured. He removed one hand from Miss Minster's waist and tried to open the offside door, but the bottom of it struck the ground after moving only a couple of inches.

"Mr. Petts, may I trouble you to try the door on your side, and see if you can summon the guard?" he asked, at which Mr. Petts heaved Mr. Tupper to one side and managed to unlatch the door and push it away, the angle of the coach making this an upward movement at first, and then gravity bringing the wide-open door with a crash to the side of the coach. He then heaved himself halfway out of the opening and bellowed "Guard?"

"Ah'm over 'ere!" replied the guard. "Can someone come and 'elp me?" Mr. Petts kicked and pulled himself clear and disappeared.

"I'll go see what's up," Jem volunteered, and struggled uphill to the open door, clambered through it and jumped to the ground, the coach rocking ominously with his movements. Presently, his hedgehog face appeared in the opening, not much above floor level.

"Gor blimey!" he explained inelegantly. "We ain't 'arf in a pickle! Bloody drag's right orf the road and 'alfway dahn a raveen. The 'orses is prancing and kicking and rolling their eyes, and the guard's 'anging on to 'em and bein' chucked abaht. The dragsman's sitting in the snow moaning, and I reckon you'd better come aht o' there afore the rock what you're leaning on gives way and sends yer right over!"

"Oh, is that all?" Sir Richard replied in a faintly sarcastic drawl. "I thought we might be in some kind of difficulty! I'll help Miss Minster to reach the doorway, and then you may be able to assist her to alight without discommoding her too much."

"Don't 'e talk lovely!" Jem said admiringly.

With Sir Richard's assistance, Miss Minster was able to reach a position where she was virtually lying on the steeply-sloping seat, and by setting her feet against his thigh—she did not remember until afterwards that it must have been his injured leg—she managed to push herself up to the open door. Jem seized her hands in a firm grip and heaved, and Sir Richard rendered further assistance, without apparently any thought of the impropriety of it, by placing one hand on her seat and giving her a good strong shove. When she was halfway out, Jem shifted his grasp to her waist, lifted her bodily and set her on her feet on the steep slope, where she sank almost to the knees in soft snow. Sir Richard tossed the rug to Jem, who folded it and put it around her shoulders.

A quick glance round showed her that the coach was lying diagonally across the slope which ran sharply down from the road to the shallow frozen stream. The driver was sitting on a rock clutching his leg and rocking to and fro, muttering vituperatively. Mr. Petts and the guard were down in the stream, splashing about amid broken ice and trying to hold on to the four terrified horses, which were bucking and prancing about and tangling themselves alarmingly in their ribbons. The coach had no visible means of support from where she was standing, to hold it in its present precarious balance, and it was only when she started to make her way towards the driver that she saw the rock which was wedged against the remains of the offside front wheel, for the moment preventing the vehicle from crashing over completely on to its side.

Meanwhile, Jem and Sir Richard had succeeded in extracting Mr. Tupper from the coach and he was looking about him in horrified bewilderment, clutching his valise and tut-tutting in agitation. Jem had to request him to move out of the way so that he could assist his master, and Miss Minster abandoned her attempt to reach the driver in order to go back and help.

Hampered by his stiff and very painful knee, Sir Richard had great difficulty in reaching the door. Eventually, Jem took off his greatcoat and upended himself headfirst through the doorway, having requested Miss Minster to take a good grip on the stout belt which supported his trousers. He then seized Sir Richard by the armpits, and with Miss Minster leaning back and hauling on his belt, succeeded in dragging him halfway out. The hilt of his sabre caught on the door frame, but once that was freed, he was able to wriggle and heave himself clear and reach firm ground, steadying himself with a hand on Miss Minster's shoulder while he surveyed the scene, breathing rather hard and very white about the mouth. Jem disappeared headfirst inside the vehicle again, and emerged with the walking-stick, gave it to his master, struggled into his coat, jammed his battered hat well down on his head, and went to cut the horses free from their traces and ribbons, which calmed them a little. He then talked to them soothingly until he was able to take them over from the guard and Mr. Petts, who returned to the coach and went into committee with Sir Richard over the situation, the guard first conscientiously checking the lock of his mailbox.

"Is the driver hurt much?" Sir Richard asked. "He appears to have injured his leg." He began to pick his way over to see, moving with great difficulty because of the steep, uneven ground and the depth of snow. The others went with him and stood round watching while he lowered himself on to his good knee, his other leg sticking out awkwardly to the side.

"What happened?" he asked.

"Ah doan't reetly know," the driver replied. "Some gurt black thing came flapping out of t'snow reet afore t'leaders—a corbie, might be. T'cattle shied and pulled to t'left, and afore Ah could pull 'em straight, we wore over t'edge, and Ah were flying through t'air. Ah reckon me ankle's busted!"

Sir Richard took off a glove and carefully felt the ankle through the supple leather of the driver's boot.

"I think not," he said. "But it's swelling a great deal, and you'll not be able to walk on it for some time. Best keep your boot on for support, and this will help as well." He rummaged under his redingote and produced his red and gold waist-sash, with which he bandaged the ankle tightly.

Mr. Petts gave him a hand to get back on to his feet, and then he looked about him at as much as could be seen in the driving snow and said reflectively, "What next?"

"What next?" exclaimed Mr. Tupper in great agitation. "Why, we must get the coach back on the road, of course! There must be no delay, or the road will have become impassable, and we shall be forced to stay here, without food or shelter!"

"I must say that I'd not much relish the thought of spending the night here," Sir Richard said soothingly, "but getting the coach back on the road is going to be a mite difficult, I fear!"

"We must summon help!" Mr. Tupper declared. "There must be someone about—shepherds, or other travellers, perhaps! We must shout for them!'' and with-out more ado, he flung back his head and screamed, "Help! Help!'' in a remarkably piercing falsetto.

The sudden blast of sound took everyone by surprise. Sir Richard started and swung round, cannoning into Mr. Petts. Miss Minster jumped and dropped her reticule, but worst of all, Jem stepped back sharply, caught his foot on a loose stone which threw him off-balance, and sat down heavily with a tremendous splash, showering the team with ice and water, just as they were flinging up their heads in alarm at Mr. Tupper's shout. They whinnied with fright and incontinently bolted, dragging the remains of their harness out of Jem's hands and disappearing al-most immediately in the thick curtain of snow.

"Oh, Gawd!'' exclaimed Jem. "Nah look what you've done! What you want to screech like that for?''

"You damn' stupid idiot!'' Sir Richard exclaimed forcefully. The guard flung his hat on the ground and fairly jittered with rage, using a number of expressions which Miss Minster had never heard before.

"Ah hev to take t'Mail on, coom what may!'' he said eventually, losing that careful veneer of educated speech. "Ah hev to take one of t'osses and go to t'next post! What for did you want to go and do a damn fool thing laike that? Now t'mail'll be late and Ah'll be fined!''

"I'm sure the Postmaster will excuse you, in view of the weather,'' Mr. Tupper said nervously. "And if not, I'll willingly pay your fine, for it was indeed my fault, and I'm very sorry for it.''

"Sorry don't 'elp much!'' the guard said bitterly. "T'Postmaster-General don't reckon snow nor rain nor nothing—t'Mail 'as to go through if it rains 'ot coals and salmagunders! Ah'll 'ave to *walk* now!''

"We'll all have to walk," Sir Richard pointed out. "The driver must be taken to shelter as soon as possible, for his ankle may be broken, and in any case, an immobile man is in real danger in this cold." He did not mention the fact which was patently clear to them all, that anyone who remained here overnight would not be likely to see the morning. "Now," he continued, "which way shall we go?"

CHAPTER THREE

"AH HEV TO go *on*," the guard said firmly. "Any case, t'road ahead is easier than going back down t'Raise."

"But it must be miles to Thirlspot!" Mr. Tupper objected.

"There's an inn at Wythburn, three-four miles on, at t'head of Leatheswater. T'Nag's 'Ead. Not a posthouse, but a fair enough place. Any road, 'tis shelter for you and a mount for me," the guard replied.

"Ah'll not get there," the driver said morosely.

"Yes you will!" Sir Richard informed him. "Jem, get out of that water and take one of the doors off its hinges! Guard, I take it you have a tool-box?"

"Indeed Ah have!" The guard sounded quite truculent, as if he thought that Sir Richard might be suggesting otherwise. "Complete as specified!"

"Good. Fetch it then, if you please!"

Mr. Petts, who had been clambering about making a circuit of the wrecked coach, interrupted with a certain gloomy relish, "We'd never 'ave got the drag back on the road—one wheel's all to pieces. Felloes are busted!"

"Then bring four of the spokes, if you please!" Sir Richard had braced himself firmly against the slope of the ground and was giving politely expressed orders with the air of a man who knows exactly what he is doing. Miss Minster, standing a little forlornly to one side, feeling both useless and helpless, took comfort from his confident manner. It was not easy to stand or move about on the slope, for it was slippery under the snow, and there was now so much of that about that any number of loose rocks made hidden traps under it, on which the unwary might turn an ankle or trip.

She found a large boulder and sat down on it, huddling in the folds of the thick rug, and watched as the four spokes were screwed to the door to make handles, and the resulting rough stretcher carried up to the road. At the same time, she was thinking how lucky they all were that Sir Richard and Jem were with them, for no one else would have known how to deal with the situation. There was something about the baronet which made her feel confident in his ability to cope with any emergency, and she was sure that she would have been terrified when the coach came off the road if she had not been caught and held so safely by him.

On reflection, she could only recall two occasions when a man had put his arms round her, apart from her father. The first had been the son of one of her father's friends, when she was about fourteen, and had been accompanied by a rather wet and sticky kiss, and the other had been much more recent, when the older brother of her recent pupil had cornered her outside the schoolroom door with amatory intent. She had escaped the first embrace by telling the boy not to be silly, and the second by stamping hard on the young gentleman's foot. Neither experience had been pleasant, whereas . . .

She did not stop to pursue that thought, but, seeing that Jem and Mr. Petts were now carrying the driver up to the road to put him on the stretcher, she scrambled after them and wrapped the warm rug round him before Jem tied him firmly in place with the remains of his team's tackle.

The guard brought his two remaining mail pouches and tied them behind the injured man so that they propped him up a little, for the door was not long enough for him to lie full length. Meanwhile, Mr. Petts muttered something to Jem, and they both went back to help Sir Richard up the slope, putting his arms round their shoulders and practically carrying him.

"Thank you," he said briefly when they set him down safely on the road. He obviously disliked having to be helped, and Miss Minster thought it must be very disagreeable for an active, energetic man to be so literally leg-tied and dependent on other people.

"Well, you'd best be off, then!" he said briskly. "The four of you should be able to carry him quite well, but you may be able to pull the contraption along like a sledge some part of the way."

"Four?" Mr. Tupper realised for the first time that he was going to be expected to act as a stretcher-bearer, but he could hardly object, as the driver's life would depend on getting him to the Nag's Head, and obviously Sir Richard and Miss Minster could not help with the task. "What will you do?" he asked, as everyone turned to look at him.

"Follow as best I can," Sir Richard replied grimly. "There's no sense in you waiting for me, for I'm bound to be rather slow. Miss Minster will go with you, of course. Jem, when you've conveyed the coachman to Wythburn, perhaps you'll be good enough to return and give me a hand?"

"We all will," Mr. Petts cut in before Jem could reply. "You'll not get far on your own. We'll come back and carry you, or bring an 'oss, and as quick as we can."

"We'll be hours, even then," Jem said doubtfully, his face creased with anxiety. "You know you can't ... We can't just *leave* you!" He looked as if he might be about to jettison the driver in order to take his master instead.

"There's nothing else to be done," Sir Richard said briskly, "The sooner you start, the sooner you'll return, so you'd best be off!" As Jem still hesitated, he added sharply, "Move off, trooper!"

Jem looked rebellious, but discipline prevailed. The four men picked up the stretcher and tried it for weight and balance. Fortunately, neither the driver nor the pouches were as heavy as they might have been, and after a little preliminary shifting of grips and wriggling by the driver to improve the balance, Jem gave a brisk, "Right— forward march!" and they set off, ploughing through the snow, which was well above their ankles, and vanished almost immediately in the thickly falling flakes, Jem's voice floating back with, "I'll be's quick's I can!"

"Go with them, m'dear," Sir Richard instructed Miss Minster.

"I'll stay with you," she replied.

"What, without a chaperon?" It was meant to be a mild joke, but it sounded distinctly hollow, so he went straight to the point and came out with the hard truth. "I'm not going to get there. I can't walk a quarter-mile on a clear road, let alone four miles in this. There's no sense in you staying with me—you'd only be risking your life to no purpose."

"I couldn't keep up with them," she replied quite truthfully. "It's very difficult to walk in such deep snow in long skirts—and they're gone—I couldn't catch up with them—and I—I'd probably get lost—and I'd be afraid on my own." Although all these were quite truthful reasons, they were also excuses. Sir Richard made no reply, but looked straight into her upturned face and raised one en- quiring eyebrow.

"I couldn't leave you here all alone," she admitted.

"I've no idea what I should say to that," he said quietly. "Obviously, it's not going to be quite as straightforward as I expected. I'd made up my mind to crawl along as far as I could, and then just go to sleep. It's said to be quite easy. Now I suppose I shall have to make shift to survive, or poor Sir Marmaduke Pheasant will blame me for the loss of a governess!"

"Partridge," Miss Minster corrected unemotionally. "Perhaps I can help you along a little."

By leaning heavily on his stick and on Miss Minster's shoulder, Sir Richard managed to walk a couple of hundred yards or so, but it was very difficult. The snow grew deeper every minute, and he had to drag his injured leg through it, being unable to lift it over the top. Miss Minster's skirts grew wet and heavy and hampered her movements, even when she became exasperated and stopped to kilt them up almost to her knees with the aid of a piece of string which Sir Richard produced from one of the various pockets of his redingote.

"One should always carry a piece of string," he observed in a manner intended to be light and humorous. "It's so useful for anchoring stray dogs, or bunching up some roses, or rabbits, or tying up a prisoner... Damn!" He had taken a step forward as he spoke, but his stick apparently slipped, his injured knee gave way under him, and he fell heavily.

Miss Minster was a slender woman with no more strength than could be expected, but somehow she managed to get him on his feet again, and together they went on a little further before pausing for a rest. The wind had increased appreciably and was throwing the icy crystals into their faces, making them feel sore and chapped, and it was difficult to see.

"It's getting colder." Sir Richard was breathing heavily from his exertions.

"The wind blows right through one," Miss Minster replied, unconsciously shrinking away from it and closer to her companion.

"Perhaps we should have stayed in the coach... No, on second thoughts, we'd have been buried, I should think, and one freezes more quickly sitting still. As long as we can keep moving, we shall be all right."

Miss Minster was beginning to wonder if she could go on much longer. The cold was sapping both her strength and her will, and every step seemed harder and less worthwhile than the last. Obviously, it was much worse for Sir Richard. He was only able to manage four or five yards now before he had to rest, and he had fallen several times, finding it harder to get up again each time.

"This is damned annoying!" he panted at the next halt. "To have survived the retreat to Corunna, only to expire on a blasted turnpike practically within sight of safety! M'sister will be damnably miffed!"

"Miffed!" Miss Minster exclaimed faintly. The word seemed extraordinarily inadequate applied to a sister's feelings on hearing of the loss of her brother!

"Yes. It'll upset all her arrangements. She'll be a man short at dinner, and at cards, and whatever else she's planned. What's more, she'll be convinced I did it on purpose! She always is when anything I'm involved in goes wrong! She's always contended it was my fault Johnny Moore was killed, 'though I wasn't within half a mile when it happened! You could still reach Wythburn, you know. Perhaps you'll meet the others on the way back."

"Shall we try to go a little further?" she replied indirectly.

He put his arm about her shoulders so that he was shielding her a little from the wind as well as leaning some of his weight on her, and they managed another few yards, but then some unevenness in the road surface threw him off-balance and they both fell. When he tried to get up, his knee had given up under the strain and would no longer support him at all.

"It's no use," he said quietly. "I'm floundered. I'm sorry, m'dear." He let out his breath on a long, shuddering sigh and let his head drop forward until it rested against her shoulder. Her eyes filled with tears as she felt the sudden relaxation of his body in acceptance of defeat, but she wiped them away with the back of one damp woollen glove and looked desperately around for anything which might give inspiration. It was very silent, except for the moaning of the wind and the whisper of the falling snow. Something massive and dark loomed through the curtain, and she realised that it was an outcrop of rock on the fellside, rising up from the verge of the road.

"There's something over there," she said. "I'll see what it is." She floundered across to it, knee-deep now in the soft surface, and found a patch of ground sheltered from the wind by the rocks and kept almost clear of snow by their overhang. At least it would provide an illusion of shelter.

When she returned to Sir Richard, he was trying to get up, and seemed to some extent to have recovered his will to live. Between them, with her pulling and his crawling, they reached the rocks and huddled into that little sheltered patch. It was appreciably less cold out of the wind.

"We must try to conserve what warmth we still have," he said, "so hang propriety!" He pulled at the buttons of his redingote with numbed fingers, managed to undo them, and then pulled Miss Minster closely against him inside the coat, which he wrapped round both of them. She tucked her head, bonnet and all, between his neck and shoulder, and oddly enough felt a little more hopeful, although reason told her that their situation was not much improved.

"The other thing we must do is keep awake," he said. "If we fall asleep, we'll die."

"Yes." She felt very drowsy.

"Talk, then!" he commanded.

"What about?"

"Anything. What's your Christian name?"

"Dorcas." She was surprised by the question.

"That's a very pretty name. I like it."

"I've always thought it rather dull."

"No, not at all! M'sister's name is Jemimah—that's dull, if you like! Downright ugly, in fact. She chooses to be called Lucinda."

Miss Minster was beginning to put together a mental picture of his sister as a somewhat spoiled and managing woman, and it seemed quite in accord with her imagined character that she should choose herself another name if she disliked her given one—a ploy which would never have occurred to Miss Minster!

After a short silence, Sir Richard said cautiously, "It's none of m'business, of course, and I've no justification for asking, so don't answer if you'd rather not, but I'm puzzled about your reason for being a governess."

"There are very few occupations open to a single lady who has to support herself," she replied. "Fortunately, I received a good education myself. The only other thing I could think of was to be a companion to an elderly lady, but I didn't know how to go about that, and besides, there was such a scandal—about—about my father, you understand, that I didn't think it likely that I would be considered suitable... My own old governess helped me, and that really determined my choice, such as it was."

"But why was it necessary for you to support yourself? I'd have thought any number of likely young fellows would have been pleased to marry you!"

"After my father—died—I ceased to be eligible," she replied flatly, only the hesitation betraying any feeling.

There was another silent period while Sir Richard tried out various phrases in his mind, and then he said hesitantly, "When I knew your father, he seemed a very cheerful man, and certainly not short of the ready."

The unasked question hung in the air for an appreciable interval, and then she said in a quiet, reflective tone, as if talking to herself, "He was very happy. He had everything he wanted, except a son. My mother was very beautiful, and he loved her dearly. He loved our home in Kent, and he enjoyed living in Society, in town or country, hunting, going round the farms..."

When she stopped speaking, Sir Richard waited to see if she would go on, almost holding his breath, and presently she resumed. "Then his world fell apart. When Austria joined the Third Coalition against Bonaparte in '05, my parents went several times to balls and parties at the Austrian embassy. Later on, when one of the Ambassador's aides returned to Vienna, my...my mother...went with him. She's married to him now, I expect, but I've not heard from her since the day she left.

"After that, my father changed. For some time, he went on as before, but he began to drink and to gamble heavily, and eventually he—he was so bad that he was never sober, and he lost more and more, and plunged more heavily, I suppose, to try to get it back... When everything had gone—the town house, the horses, all the estates, and eventually even our home—he—he shot himself.''

Her voice faded away. Sir Richard said nothing, but he shifted slightly, drew her even closer and more comfortably into his embrace, and gently kissed her cheek, and thereby conveyed more understanding and sympathy than any words could have expressed.

Presently he said, ''Was there no-one you could turn to for help? No relative or friend?''

''No, only my governess. I'd no close relations, and somehow the people we had thought were friends dropped away when Father's drunkenness became an embarrassment. About a year after he—died—I met a lady in Maidstone who was our neighbour in the old days, and often used to visit our house, as we did hers. I spoke to her, but she—she cut me! It was very hurtful.''

''I wish I'd known, when did it happen?''

Assuming that he was referring to her father's suicide, she replied ''A little over four years ago.''

''In 1810. I was in the Peninsula, but I might have been able to help in some way...''

''Why should you?''

''Well, as I said, he was kind to me. Besides, I'm a born interferer in other people's lives, as you've probably noticed!''

Miss Minster was so unaccountably comforted by his reaction to her story, that she actually smiled a little at that.

The heavy overcast was now merging quite quickly into the early winter dusk, and the illusion of comparative warmth they had felt on finding some protection from the wind had long given way to a creeping chill which slowed the blood and made movement or thought increasingly difficult and burdensome. Sir Richard realised the danger, and when they had been silent for several minutes, he forced himself to make the effort to talk, rambling on inconsequentially about various adventures which had befallen him in the Peninsula, most of them with a touch of absurdity and recounted as jokes against himself. Once or twice he broke off and changed tack, having wandered into a tale not entirely suitable for the ears of a young lady. He frequently threw in a question, and if Miss Minster was slow in answering, he shook her quite roughly to make sure she was not drifting into sleep.

When he ran out of anecdotes about his own experiences, he dredged up a few about the Marquess of Wellington, for whom he obviously had considerable admiration. Miss Minster found it all very interesting, opening up a glimpse of a way of life very different from her own restricted experience.

Eventually, however, his fund of conversation ran out. In the silence which followed, Miss Minster tried to think of something to say, but nothing occurred to her, and even the effort of thinking was fast becoming too great. She drifted into a state between sleeping and waking, and lost track of the passing of time.

Presumably something must have roused her, but she did not know what it was. She opened her eyes and could not see anything at first, nor recall where she was, but after a few seconds, she remembered and forced herself to sit up and look about her.

It had stopped snowing, and a few stars could be glimpsed fleetingly through rents in the fast-moving clouds. A glimmer of light reflected from the snow and showed a desolate scene which made her feel desperately lonely and afraid. She had no idea how long a time had passed since Sir Richard stopped talking, and it was too dark to see him as anything more than a darker shape, but he seemed to be very still. She touched his face, trying to feel some warmth in it, but her hands were too numb, and it was only by putting her own cheek close to his lips that she was able to tell that he was still breathing. For a moment, she was tempted to sink back into his arms and let her consciousness slip away, but instead, she made herself shake and pummel him, trying to wake him.

"Lie down, sweetheart!" he murmured, stirring. "It's not morning yet!" She went on banging her fists against his chest, and was about to give up in despair when he suddenly pulled her down on top of him and kissed her full on the mouth, sleepily at first, then with increasing awareness as he woke up. His hand slid up to cup and squeeze her breast, and the effect was so very pleasant that she was too startled to resist.

After a few moments, he brought the kiss to a gentle conclusion, removed his hand, and said "Dorcas?" in a questioning tone.

"It's—it's stopped snowing," she said in a very unsteady voice.

"Where the hell are we?" He heaved himself up on one elbow and looked about him, and then apparently recovered his memory, for he answered himself with, "Oh, yes the gentle, temperate climate of England! Of course! Isn't it about time Jem arrived to rescue us?"

"I don't know how long we've been here," Miss Minster replied despondently. The effort of waking him seemed to have drained her last reserve of strength.

"Sit up!" he commanded. "Come, we've survived thus far—it can't be very much longer now!" He took her by the shoulders and pulled her up beside him, propping her against the rock which provided their shelter. As he did so, a voice called "Sir?" from somewhere not far off, echoing across the narrow pass.

"Thank God! Jem!" Sir Richard murmured, and then repeated the name with as much force as he could muster. It emerged as a very feeble effort at shouting, but it brought an answering bellow from much closer, and within minutes, Jem loomed up against the faint snow-glimmer, swinging a lantern which sent grotesque shadows dancing round him. Miss Minster, thinking only hazily and with difficulty, was puzzled by them at first, but they soon resolved themselves into two men and a heavy horse harnessed to a sledge. One of the men stepped into the light, revealing the lugubrious ear-flap-framed face of Mr. Petts, and the other appeared to be a stranger.

She had no real recollection of what happened after that, only disjointed images of being cocooned in blankets and of gliding along, with an occasional jolt, as the horse tramped steadily down the long hill to Wythburn, dragging the sledge over the crisp surface, while someone chafed her hands and feet, of lights and voices, and being carried up some stairs, and eventually of sinking into a yielding surface which was warm, and feeling a wonderful glow as the heat from two or three sources close about her flowed into her body.

When she woke again, it was daylight, and a peculiarly cold, hard sort of daylight at that, reflecting on a white-washed plaster ceiling from low double-casement windows. She was lying on a plain wooden bed with a feather mattress, between sheets smelling of lavender and covered by thick blankets and a patchwork quilt. A tallboy stood in the corner by the window, with a mirror-stand and a jug and basin on top of it, her clothes were neatly folded on the seat of a windsor-backed rocking chair, a large rag rug covered the area of board floor in front of the fireplace, where a metal guard was set before a brightly-burning wood fire—a luxury which she had not enjoyed for many years, and her own small trunk stood between the door and a tall hanging-cupboard.

As she sat up in bed to take a better look round, there was a light tap at the door, and a plump maidservant with a capacious flower-printed apron over her thick woollen dress and a frilled mobcap on her dark curls, came in with a can of hot water. She gave Miss Minster a shy smile, and put the can down in the hearth to keep warm. When she spoke, Miss Minster had great difficulty in understanding what she said, for her northern accent was very pronounced, but it appeared to amount to an announcement that she could take breakfast down in the parlour if she felt able to get up, that it looked as if more snow was likely, and that she was in the Nag's Head inn at Wythburn by Leatheswater.

When the girl had gone, Miss Minster got out of bed and went to look out of the window, discovering as she did so that she was wearing a white nightshift obviously made for a much larger female, for it hung in folds about her slender figure and even trailed on the ground a little.

The view from the window was impressive, majestic, and made her feel a little depressed, for she found that she was looking across a stableyard with grey stone walls and buildings down a long snow-covered slope to a great expanse of frozen water which stretched away to her right until it vanished from sight beyond some trees about a mile away. Beyond the lake, the ground rose gradually at first and dotted with clumps of black trees, and then reared up steeply into a great ridge like a giant feather-bolster, which blotted most of the sky, leaving only a narrow strip of leaden clouds between the highest crags and the top of the window-frame. The whole scene was deep in snow, and presented a harsh picture in stark black, grey and white.

She turned away from it with a shiver and hastened to wash herself while the water was still warm. Her linen, she found, had been washed and ironed, and the dark red dress she had worn the previous day had been dried and brushed and pressed. It was quite fit to wear, but she hung it in the cupboard, where she found her cloak, redingote and bonnet, also dried and brushed, and instead put on another dress from her truck, a dark blue trimmed with a little black braiding round the high waist and stiffened neckband. Then she brushed her hair and pinned it in place. One little strand broke loose and formed a curl by her left ear, and after a brief hesitation, she left it, thinking it not unbecoming, and feeling that she need not adhere strictly to the severity of appearance expected of a governess until she arrived at her new place. A shawl completed her toilette, in case it should be draughty in the rooms downstairs, and then she was ready to go down.

She found that the door of her room opened on to a landing, with four or five more doors at intervals. Opposite the one immediately to the right of her own, a flight of stairs ran up to the next floor, and another flight descended next to them to the ground floor.

Standing at the top of the downward flight, she listened for a moment, and heard voices somewhere below—a man apparently telling some tale, and then a woman's laugh, very hearty and filled with life. She walked down the stairs and found herself in a stone-flagged entrance-hall. At the far end, facing her, was the front door, closed, with a fanlight over it. A door to the right stood half-open, and another on the left was shut. A passage ran back beside the stairs, presumably to the kitchen regions. The walls were whitewashed and hung with a few framed prints and a hunting-horn, with a rack of wooden pegs by the front door, one of which supported a small horse-collar, and another a beaver-hat and a dark cloak.

She went to the half-open door and looked into the room, which had a bare, scrubbed stone floor, and a large stone fireplace with a log fire crackling in it. A dozen or so wooden tables with benches and stools were set about the room, faded but clean chintz curtains hung at the window, and the opposite end of the room was occupied by a wooden counter, behind which some shelves supported bottles and mugs, and a barrel stood on its side on a wooden support, with a spigot set in its lid. Presumably this was the tap-room.

Miss Minster left the door ajar, as she had found it, and tried the room opposite. This was smaller, and the curtains at the window were newer and brighter in colour. A rectangular table of dark wood, polished mirror-bright, with hoop-backed chairs set about it, occupied the centre of the room, and opposite the door was another big stone fireplace, with a guard to protect the rag rug from the spitting logs. Above it hung a glazed and framed print of King George III in his younger and happier days, looking somewhat dyspeptic and with a sinister cast in one eye, due, presumably, to the artist's ineptitude.

This room was also empty, but another door opened from it at the end furthest from the window, and this proved to be the entrance to a cosy parlour, bright with copper jugs on the window-sill, wool-embroidered cushions on the chairs, pretty curtains, two or three colourful rag rugs on the stone floor, and a high-backed settle by a roaring fire. Sir Richard was sitting in a straight-backed chair with a small table at his elbow and his injured leg propped up on a stool, reading a book. He looked up as she entered, laid aside his book and reached for his stick, obviously intending to rise.

"Oh, pray don't get up!" Miss Minster said quickly, and he subsided again without argument. On closer inspection, he looked pale and drawn, and his knee was obviously paining him. They exchanged a formal "Good morning."

"I trust you are none the worse for yesterday's calamities m'dear?" he added, and Miss Minster assured him that she was in good health. "But I think your leg troubles you?" she asked.

"It don't take kindly to rampaging about in the snow and being fell on," he replied ungrammatically, and she had to repress a governessish impulse to correct him, which, together with a realisation that he had now called her "m'dear" several times, quite improperly, of course, and she should really give him a set-down before he assumed she had no objection, caused her colour to rise suddenly.

"It was a much less pleasant awakening this morning, finding myself sharing a room with Jem, who snores abominably, and m'knee making its displeasure felt," he continued. Miss Minster caught the mischievous gleam in his eye, realised what he meant, and coloured up even more, wondering at what point in the process of waking up just before Jem's arrival last night he had realised who it was shaking him.

"Have you taken breakfast?" he asked suddenly, and when she replied in the negative, he picked up a little handbell from his table and rang it vigorously.

After a couple of minutes, Jem came in, and greeted Miss Minster with a cheerful, "Good Morning!" then looked expectantly at his master, like a dog hoping someone was going to throw a stick.

"Breakfast for Miss Minster, please Jem," Sir Richard said briskly. "And where have all the others disappeared to?"

"Mr. Tupper's still abed, for fear 'e might 'ave taken cold," Jem replied without much expression. "Mr. Petts 'as gone with Mr. Black to see if the road's blocked along the lake, and Mr. Kirby's sitting in the stable moaning over 'is 'orse, which ain't doing a lot o' good. Dragsman's snug by the kitchen fire."

"And the guard?" Miss Minster enquired.

"Oh, 'e went strite on last night. 'Ired a mount from 'ere and rode orf like a rigimint o' Chasseurs!" With that, he departed, and Miss Minster drew up a chair to the opposite side of Sir Richard's table, and asked, "Pray, who are Mr. Black and Mr. Kirby?"

"Both stranded travellers, like ourselves," Sir Richard replied, stacking up the four or five books on the table to make more room. "Black is another Londoner, not unlike Mr. Petts, who was heading for Kendal, but was lucky to get thus far, and Mr. Kirby is one of the local squires, who was riding ahead of us, going home to Keswick, but his mount went lame and he decided to stop here. Just as well, for if he'd hired the only riding horse they keep here, I don't know how the guard would have managed. It appears that Mr. Kirby's horse is a blood mare, and he's very concerned about her—he's been sitting up with her as if she's a sick relative!"

"Is the horse badly injured?"

"Jem says not. He could probably set her to rights with one of his magic poultices, but when he offered his assistance Mr. Kirby was rather rude to him and called him an amateur horse-leech, so Jem has taken offence!"

Another plump maid arrived with a tray, from which she set a place for Miss Minster on the table and offered her an imposing selection of breakfast dishes, from which she chose a couple of thick, juicy slices of fried ham, an egg and some toast, and set to with a good appetite, having had nothing since luncheon at Grasmere Town Head the day before, until she recalled the state of her finances, and suddenly lost her desire for food.

"Do you think we shall have to stay here long?" she asked, her anxious look returning.

"I fear so. If the guard managed to get through to Keswick, presumably he will return with a relief coach as soon as the road becomes passable, but it snowed heavily again in the night, and a further fall seems imminent this morning. The Boniface here says that the road has been impassable for a vehicle since yesterday afternoon, with some very deep drifts, and he doubts if even a horse could have got through by this morning. I pray the guard was able to reach safety—he was obviously a very conscientious fellow, who would make every effort to deliver his mailbags, even at the risk of his life. But to return to your question—it looks as if we shall be here for Christmas, and until such time as there is a thaw thereafter, which could be a couple of days or several weeks." He looked at her worried face and added, "If it's the cost that concerns you, you know I'd be happy to help."

"You're very kind. I have a horror of falling into debt, but... but I fear I may have to accept your offer," she replied unsteadily. "Only if I really must, of course."

"Of course," he agreed, and did not press the point for the moment. She had already progressed a long way from the polite refusal of luncheon-time yesterday. He busied himself with pouring her some tea.

CHAPTER FOUR

CONVERSATION LAPSED whilst Miss Minster ate her breakfast, and presently she began to feel that the silence had become something of a barrier, so while she was drinking her second dish of tea, she cast about in her mind for a neutral topic, and eventually said, "So you will be unable to reach your sister's home in time for Christmas after all."

"Yes, and she'll not be best pleased!" he replied ruefully. "On the other hand, she'll be relieved to find that she need not go into mourning for me—she much dislikes wearing black—it don't suit her."

"There may be a thaw in a day or two, to enable you to enjoy some of the festivities, at least."

"Enjoy? Endless games of whist and idle chatter with a bevy of wallflowers?" He sounded as if the prospect was far from pleasing.

"Wallflowers?"

"Yes. I gather that m'sister's concluded it to be past time for me to marry, and she's collected me a selection of fairly plain young ladies, any one of whom she thinks might be prepared to accept me."

"But why?"

He picked up one of his books, opened it at the beginning, and replied to her question in the words of that anonymous author who was later to be revealed as Miss Austen, "'It is a truth universally acknowledged that a single man in possession of a good fortune, must be in want of a wife!' She's right—I'll be thirty next birthday, and the estates are entailed—the heir at the moment is some incredibly distant cousin—but I don't much relish the prospect of a plain, dull, bread-and-butter miss.'' He sounded bitter.

"Why should you have to make do with such an one? I should think most people would consider you a most eligible *parti*!''

"It can't have escaped your notice that I'm a cripple. I can't imagine that an attractive female would wish to be shackled to a man who can't dance, or even walk properly. Besides, you must have noticed that in all the most fashionable novels, if a lame man appears, he's invariably a villain. In real life, too—Lord Barrymore, Byron, even the Devil himself!''

"I think you are quite wrong!'' Miss Minster informed him in spirited tones, nettled that he should assume that all her sex would be so stupid as to spurn a good man simply because he happened to be a trifle lame.

Sir Richard contemplated her face for a few seconds, looking a little perturbed and puzzled, and then said abruptly, "I rather think you saved my life last night, and I've not yet thanked you.''

Miss Minster busied herself in piling her used crockery on the tray and replied, "It was as much the other way about, and I should thank you,'' and then rang the little handbell, bringing Jem in almost immediately and thus preventing any further discussion of the matter.

"I've fahnd yer a book o' four kings and a box o' poxbones,'' Jem informed his master, depositing a pack of old playing-cards and a box of dominoes on the table. "Yer can play thumpers if you've a mind.''

"How did my trunk get here from the coach?" Miss Minster asked him.

"I went up 'smorning, early, soon as it stopped blizzarding, with the groom from 'ere and the 'orse and sledge, and we digged the baggage aht."

"That was kind of you, thank you. Was it very difficult?"

"Nah, but the snow's real deep up there, an' the 'ighest bit, beyond the drag, was blocked right up, so there's no going back, and Mr. Petts just come in says it's blocked up a'ead as well, so 'ere we are 'til it melts! Still, it's snug 'ere—good grub an' clean beds. Couldn't want a better billet, and no Scots Greys nor Light Bobs quartered wiv us, neether!"

"Scots Greys . . . ?" Miss Minster queried faintly, half-guessing.

"Bugs and fleas," Sir Richard translated apologetically. "That will do, Jem, thank you!"

Jem grinned unashamedly and made off with Miss Minster's tray, leaving the door open behind him, and a moment later, Mr. Petts entered with another man, like enough to him to have been his brother, except that where Mr. Petts tended to look mournful, the newcomer had a permanent half-smile which a broken front tooth contrived to turn into something of a leer.

"'Enery Black!" he announced, giving Miss Minster a flourishing bow, and Mr. Petts grudgingly told him her name.

"I hear you've been investigating conditions along the lakeside," Sir Richard said. "How does it look?"

"Middling 'opeless!" Mr. Black replied, pulling a chair up to the fire and sprawling in it, booted legs sticking out towards the heat, and hooking his dark blue coat back to hitch his thumbs in the pockets of a striped red and green waistcoat. "'Though I reckon a drag with a six-team might manage the first bit. After the causey, even oxen wouldn't get through. It's a great nuisance, and I resents the waste of me time it occasions!"

"Oh, you're a man of business, then?" Sir Richard sounded a little amused at the man appearing to take the weather as a personal affront.

"In a manner of speaking. I 'as business 'ereabouts, and my business is to ask *questions*, but I can't ask me questions when I'm stuck 'ere in this flea-kennel, can I?"

"What sort of questions?" Sir Richard asked curiously.

"Oh, 'oo rides aht at night, and 'oo gets robbed, and 'oo might be worth robbing next, not ter mention 'oo does the robbing!"

"Are you a thief-taker, then?" Sir Richard enquired with great interest.

"Thief-taker! You don't call a Bow Street Runner a mere thief-taker, do yer, cully? Not just a common or garden *thief-taker*!"

Mr. Petts, who had picked up a couple of Sir Richard's books and was looking at their titles, knocked the whole pile on the floor, and had to go down on his hands and knees to retrieve them, muttering an apology as he did so, but Sir Richard said that it didn't matter, and generously offered the loan of any volume which he fancied, which led to him retiring to the settle and becoming immersed in a handsomely-bound copy of *The Bride of Abydos*, which seemed to Miss Minster a surprising choice.

Mr. Black, meanwhile, was enlarging on his profession, and recounted several tales of criminals he had known, showing a charitable touch of admiration for the cleverness and audacity of some of them. His talk was so larded with cant expressions that Miss Minster found it almost incomprehensible, and soon gave up listening, seeking permission to borrow one of Sir Richard's books herself by means of a gesture and an inquiring look, to which he replied by pushing them across the table to her to take her choice. As she had not yet had an opportunity to read the latest publication of the author of *Sense and Sensibility*, she opened *Pride and Prejudice* and was soon lost in the problems of the Misses Bennet.

Luncheon was served in the dining-room next door, and they were all about to sit down to it when Mr. George Kirby made his entrance, and was duly made known to Miss Minster.

He was a remarkably handsome young man of twenty-five or so, with thick golden hair, fine blue eyes, and a very pleasant, if slightly gushing, manner. He apologised for appearing in riding-dress, but explained that he had ridden over to Ambleside from Keswick the day before, intending to return home in the evening, and had only a change of linen with him as a precaution in case he was delayed overnight.

"You live in Keswick, then?" Miss Minster enquired, surprised to find that he lacked any trace of the north in his speech.

"Just beyond the town, but I'm not a native of these parts," he replied. "My real home is in Hertfordshire, but I inherited a tidy estate up here from an uncle, and find it convenient to live here most of the year. The sport is first-rate, you see—plenty of hunting, shooting, fishing and so on, and the estate's been a bit neglected, so I shall have to keep a close eye on things for a while."

"Do you like living in this part of the world?" Miss Minster asked. Something in her voice made Sir Richard give her a sharp, searching look, and reflect that she must be very doubtful about her own commitment to live in the Lake District, now she had seen the worst of it.

"Oh, it's well enough, for country amusements, but I miss the distractions of London—theatres, clubs and so on, you know."

"Actresses and gambling, you mean!" Sir Richard thought uncharitably, having taken a totally unreasoning dislike to the young man.

Luncheon was a comparatively light meal, consisting of a selection of dishes of coddled eggs, cold beef, ham, roots and cabbage, followed by a loaf of new bread, a mild cheese and a gooseberry pie. By the time it was finished, the promise of the morning had been fulfilled, and it was again snowing. Mr. Black and Mr. Petts removed themselves to the taproom, Mr. Kirby fidgetted about for a while, and then went back to the stable, and Sir Richard and Miss Minster returned to the parlour, where he gave her a little elementary instruction in the mysteries of thumpers.

Some time later, Mr. Kirby rejoined them, and said that the snow had not stopped, and some of the servants were digging their way across the road to the little stone chapel which served the Leatheswater valley. He obligingly joined in the playing of thumpers, but obviously found it rather dull, and presently suggested a small wager on the result of each game.

"I don't gamble," Sir Richard replied firmly.

"What, not at all? Good Lord! You ain't a Methody, are you?"

"I'm a practicing Anglican," Sir Richard replied in a tone which strongly implied that it was none of Mr. Kirby's business. "And as far as I'm aware, there is no law which forbids an Anglican from abstaining from gambling."

Mr. Kirby was clearly at a loss to account for this eccentricity, but he accepted with a shrug and continued to play, as there was nothing else much to do.

At a little before five o'clock, Miss Minster decided to change for dinner, and excused herself. Halfway across the dining-room, she realised that she had left her shawl on the back of her chair, for she had not needed it, started back to get it, but as she reached the door, she was arrested with her hand on the knob by the sound of Mr. Kirby saying her own name. The latch had not quite caught, and the door was slightly ajar.

"This Miss Minster," Mr. Kirby was saying. "Is she—er—travelling with you?"

"In what sense?" enquired Sir Richard in a singularly expressionless voice.

"Well, you know—under your—er—protection."

There was a slight pause, and then Sir Richard replied coldly, "I happened to board the cross-mail at Keswick because my own conveyance had met with an accident. Miss Minster happened to board the same cross-mail, as did Mr. Petts and Mr. Tupper."

"Oh. So she ain't with you?"

"She is not 'with' anyone, in the sense you imply."

"She doesn't appear to have even a maid with her, though—a bit fishy, what?"

"Some people can find a whiff of Billingsgate in anything, if they try."

"Meaning?"

"That you would do better to enquire the real reason for Miss Minster to be travelling alone before leaping to any conclusions."

"Oh. What's the real reason, then?" Mr. Kirby still sounded agreeable and friendly, in contrast to Sir Richard's icy tones.

"The lady happens to be a governess, travelling to a new appointment. I should not imagine that any governess is able to afford the services of a maid, or hire a duenna."

"A governess! Oh, well—she's quite an attractive piece, in a quiet sort of way—rather restful, in fact. If you ain't established a claim, I suppose she's fair game, then?"

"I would not describe a lady of unimpeachable birth, breeding and morals as 'fair game' under any circumstances!" Sir Richard replied with such steely coldness that even Mr. Kirby's obviously thick skin was pierced by it, and he replied "Oh!" in a suitably chastened manner.

Miss Minster pressed cold hands to her burning cheeks and fled upstairs to her room, where she indulged in a few tears of mortification. She had hated the idea of travelling so far alone, having some fear that it might lead to problems of this nature. She found Mr. Kirby's misapprehension quite understandable, and could not blame him for it, for it was an inescapable, if regrettable, fact that a female travelling unchaperoned was in a very unconventional situation.

She was not given to wasting regrets on what could not be helped, and very quickly told herself to stop being foolish, washed her face, changed her dress and tidied herself, and in due course went down to dinner with her usual expression of calm composure, comforting herself with the thought that Sir Richard had taken the trouble to defend her reputation when he might quite easily have drawn conclusions about her similar to Mr. Kirby's, in view of the fact that she had made no further protest at his habit of addressing her as "m'dear".

It happened that as she was tidying her hair, she had paid it so little attention that two or three more curls had escaped, and when she entered the dining-room, Sir

Richard, who happened to be nearest the door, held her chair for her and took the opportunity to say quietly, "You know, Dorcas, your hair is very pretty. You should let it curl like that all the time."

In view of her thoughts on the way downstairs, it is hardly surprising that she replied to this unwarranted familiarity with a severely downsetting "Colonel Severall!" looking him straight in the face with every appearance of indignation.

He looked at her in some surprise for a moment, then a gleam which could have been anger or amusement appeared in his eyes, and he replied "Miss Minster!" and acknowledged her implied reprimand with a slight bow. She then, of course, recalled his recent defense of her reputation, and felt perversely that she was being very unfair to him.

The room had been decorated with holly and coloured ribbons during the afternoon, and looked very festive, and the dinner was excellent, with beefsteak pie, a very sweet saddle of mutton with redcurrant jelly, boiled potatoes, cabbage and pease-pudding, followed by substantial slices of suet pudding, which one of the maids said was called "cowed leady". Mr. Black complained about the lack of side-dishes, and the limited choice, and the absence of oysters from the pie, but received no support, all the others remarking pointedly on the good quality of the food, and its difference from that usually served in inns. The gentlemen took a pint of port apiece, and some pleasant sweet canary was found for Miss Minster, at Sir Richard's suggestion.

"Wery suitable!" Mr. Black observed with a smirk, and, as Miss Minster was not acquainted with the cant meaning of "canary-bird", the jibe passed unnoticed by her, but not by Sir Richard, who scowled.

Sounds of merriment and voices uplifted in song attracted Mr. Petts and Mr. Black back to the taproom after dinner, where they found a dozen or so locals had somehow struggled in to the Nag's Head, although goodness knew from where, for there was no other habitation in sight. The others returned to the parlour, where Mr. Kirby, still worried about his horse, applied to Sir Richard for advice.

"I—er—wondered—I believe you may be a cavalryman?" he began, looking doubtfully at Sir Richard's expanse of gold braid.

"Dragoon," he replied.

"Oh. Er—is that cavalry?"

Sir Richard appeared amused by his ignorance and replied quite kindly, "Well, originally we were mounted infantry, but now we count as Heavy Cavalry."

"*Heavy* cavalry?"

"As opposed to Light Cavalry. That means we are big men on big horses, with cuirasses and helmets, and when we crash *en masse* into an enemy formation, we leave them feeling they've been tolled on by an elephant."

Miss Minster began to laugh at the description, caught Sir Richard's eye, and received a very friendly wink, which was a relief as she had feared that her earlier setdown might have offended him.

"Oh, I see. Then you know a bit about horses?" Mr. Kirby continued.

"A little. They have four legs each, a head at the front and a tail at the back, and come in various colours, or spots, but never, to my knowledge, stripes. If you're concerned about your mare, you should let Jem have a look." Sir Richard had grown tired of Mr. Kirby's longwinded approach.

"The trouble is, she's a very valuable animal. Half-Arab, with a first-rate pedigree. I suppose your man is used to ordinary nags?"

Sir Richard winced slightly, his own *remuda* having been the envy of many brother-officers with an eye to blood-stock, but he replied equably, "If it's horse-shaped, Jem is used to it, regardless of weight, size or pedigree. He has the gift, you see—the horse will tell him what's amiss, and then he'll know how to help."

"Oh, he's got a frog-bone, has he?" Apparently enlightenment had dawned on Mr. Kirby.

"I don't know the secret, but whatever it is, Jem has got it," Sir Richard declared. "I'll ask him to take a look in the morning, but you'll have to make it clear that you're aware that he's not an amateur horse-leech!"

Mr. Kirby looked guilty at hearing his careless opinion thrown back at him, but he had the grace to say that he would put that right at the first opportunity, and thanked Sir Richard effusively, then turned his attention to entertaining Miss Minster. She was a little ill-at-ease about this at first, remembering the conversation she had overheard, but his attitude was so unexceptionable that she concluded that he had taken Sir Richard's correction about herself as well, and could not help responding to his very considerable charm, and blossomed herself into a very attractive young lady in the warmth of this unaccustomed and flattering attention. By the time she retired for the night, she thought him a very pleasant and kindly young man, and most obliging to take so much trouble to engage in conversation with a mere governess. In fact, she was so bedazzled by his good looks and lulled by his friendly manner, that she had not noticed that Sir Richard had sat with his nose in a book all evening, not joining in the conversation at all. If she had given it any thought, she would have assumed that his knee was painful and made him disinclined to talk.

Her featherbed was pleasantly warm when she climbed into it, due to the presence of a hot brick wrapped in flannel, and she slept very well, waking in the morning with an unusual feeling of happy anticipation, as if the day might bring some special happening. It was several minutes before she remembered that it was Christmas Day.

The chambermaid brought her watercan, wished her a Merry Christmas, and lit her fire, and when she dressed, she took out from her trunk the one good evening dress she had kept from the old days, and hung it up to let the creases drop out, thinking that she might change into it for dinner.

On her way downstairs, she came upon Jem, kissing one of the maids under the large kissing-bunch which hung from a convenient beam at the foot of the stairs. They were both too engrossed to notice Miss Minster's arrival, and Jem seemed to be having much his own way in the matter, despite the fact that the girl was halfheartedly pummelling his shoulders with her clenched fists, and kicking at his ankles with her heavy shoes, but not actually making any connection.

"Here Jem! Leave some for others!" said Sir Richard from behind her, and leaned past her to prod his man in the ribs with his stick. Jem surfaced for air, and the girl took the opportunity to wriggle free and ran off towards the kitchen, giggling.

"Not so 'ot-blooded as the seenoritas, but a fair sight cleaner!" was Jem's verdict, and then he politely wished Miss Minster the compliments of the season before following the girl towards the back of the house.

Miss Minster bade Sir Richard "Good morning," as he opened the door of the dining-room for her, and he replied gravely, adding "Miss Minster" with a slight smile, at which she gave him an uncertain look, wondering if he was making fun of her for setting him down the previous evening, and decided that he was, for as he followed her into the room, he added under his breath, "Yes, very pretty indeed!"

Mr. Black was already seated at the table, idly spinning a knife. He made a perfunctory gesture towards rising and replied to the new arrivals' greetings with a brusque "Morning" then added "I s'pose we'll get fed some time, 'though there's no sign of grub so far."

"It's still quite early, and the folk here are not used to so many guests at one time," Sir Richard replied. "I believe most of their trade is in the summer, with people wishing to walk in the area, or to climb Helvellyn." He was standing near the head of the table, which he had taken the previous day, leaning on his stick and looking with interest at a large marmalade cat, which rose from the hearthrug and came to sniff his boots.

Miss Minster went to the window and stood looking out at the snow-covered road, the little chapel beyond it, with a narrow pathway dug through the drifts to its door, and the great ridge rising above it. The sun had not yet risen above the fell, but the sky was a clear pale blue, and the scene was less forbidding than it had seemed the previous day.

The cat apparently decided that Sir Richard was a person worthy of recognition, and rubbed its head against his leg, purring loudly, and Miss Minster, her attention caught by the sound, turned to see the tall soldier bending to scratch the animal behind its ears, a process which was obviously to its liking.

"Dratted animal!" Mr. Black said, scowling.

"You're a remarkably handsome fellow, ain't you?" Sir Richard said to the cat, which clearly agreed with him.

Mr. Petts, Mr. Kirby and Mr. Tupper entered in quick succession, and there was a general exchange of greetings and seasonal wishes, and then Mr. Kirby gravitated to Miss Minster's side, but she was too busy enquiring after Mr. Tupper's health to notice at first.

"I am thankful to say that I did not take cold after all," the solicitor informed her earnestly. "I really would recommend any one who feels that they have been in the slightest danger of taking cold to go to bed *at once*! It's the only thing, you know!"

"Prosy old fellow!" Mr. Kirby murmured. Miss Minster gave him a reproving look and moved back towards the table, where Sir Richard momentarily abandoned his new friend to hold her chair while she seated herself. Mr. Kirby promptly took the place on her right, and she thus found herself between him and Sir Richard, who sat down sideways and resumed his communication with the cat. Mr. Petts took the place opposite Miss Minster and next to Mr. Black, leaving Mr. Tupper the foot of the table.

A great rattling of crockery heralded the arrival of breakfast, which was brought in by the two maids and Jem, and a pleasant array of covered dishes was soon distributed about the table, together with a couple of racks of toast and two teapots.

"'Ere, you ain't supposed to be in with the Gentry!" Jem informed the cat. "Come 'ere, Tiddles—there's a nice bit o' pig's liver in the kitchen for yer!"

"Tiddles!" exclaimed Sir Richard in scandalised tones. "Quite unworthy of such a splendid beast!"

"'Is name's Maurice, but 'e don't answer to it!" Jem replied darkly, scooping the cat up in his arms. It swarmed up him and arranged itself round the back of his neck like a large ginger muffler, and Jem transferred his attention to Mr. Kirby and said, "I've pulticed yer mare, but she'll 'ave ter lay up five-six days," in quite a kindly tone.

Mr. Kirby thanked him, but when he and the maid had withdrawn, he commented, "That man of yours is a bit of an oddity, ain't he? Wherever did you find him?"

"Halfway down a precipice in northern Spain," Sir Richard replied, offering Miss Minster a dish of cutlets, and serving himself with two after she had declined. "I was falling off it at the time, and he kindly prevented me from reaching the bottom. I'm afraid he's something of a public disaster from the conversational point of view, but he's a very capable, honest, willing fellow, and one can't have everything."

"Reckon 'e does most of it a purpose," Mr. Petts remarked, and then scowled fiercely at Miss Minster and continued reprovingly, "I 'ope you're going to 'ave more to eat than that scrap o' toast, young lady!"

To Miss Minster's confusion, everyone looked at her, and both Sir Richard and Mr. Kirby offered her ham, the already rejected cutlets, cold mutton and the remains of the beefsteak pie in quick succession, while Mr. Tupper informed her that he really would advise her to take a good, substantial breakfast in this cold weather. Mr. Black sniffed and put most of a fried egg in his mouth, followed immediately by a draught of the ale he had ordered instead of tea.

"I thought perhaps I might have an egg on the toast," Miss Minster said, a little taken aback by this unaccustomed attention. Mr. Petts at once scooped the eggs from under Mr. Black's nose, just as he was looking into the dish with a view to taking another himself, and served

Miss Minster with two, placing them neatly on her slices of toast.

"I gather there is to be a reading of Matins in the chapel this morning," Sir Richard informed the company at large. "Jem tells me that they have only a cavalry curate hereabouts, and it is the turn of another chapel to have his attendance today, but one of the churchwardens will read the service. I thought I might go—I don't know if anyone else might wish to do so?"

He looked at Miss Minster, who replied at once. "Oh, yes—I'd like to attend. It wouldn't seem like Christmas without church."

"I'll come," Mr. Kirby said a little too promptly. Mr. Tupper thought it better to stay indoors, in view of the sharp frost, Mr. Petts said, "No, thankee," and Mr. Black, having his mouth full, merely shook his head.

There was some speculation about the length of time they were all likely to have to remain at the Nag's Head, and Mr. Kirby having disclaimed any ability to foretell the local weather, having resided in Cumberland for little more than a year, Mr. Tupper volunteered the information that the first snow of winter usually lay for only a few days, followed by a quick thaw, and that longer-lasting bad weather would not begin until early January.

"In fact," he concluded, "I believe the wind has swung more westerly already."

They were distracted from the hopeful prognostication by the entry of Jem, who flung open the door with a great flourish and bowed in their hostess. She was a stout, benevolent-looking countrywoman in a very clean cap and apron, and she carried a dish in which reposed something which she said was a local delicacy called hack pudding, eaten only on Christmas morning, and composed of sheep's heart chopped up and mixed with suet, currants and raisins and boiled in a cloth. The guests each accepted a slice and tried it with caution, but it proved to be very good, and the gentlemen were not averse to a second helping.

The landlady then asked anxiously if they would object to a light luncheon, as dinner in the evening would be something special. She was reassured by a pleasant speech from Sir Richard, thanking her for the warmth of her hospitality to the unexpected horde which had descended on her, and she went out beaming with relief.

"Ain't bad, that 'ack pudding," Jem remarked, looking round to see if anyone was in need of anything. "Better nor a bang on the back wiv a brick, any'ow!"

"Jem," said his master quietly, "Mum your dubber and go polish my helmet, or something!"

"Sir!" replied the servant woodenly, and went out looking dramatically offended, while Sir Richard shook his head and grinned ruefully at Miss Minster.

"I must apologise for his infelicitous remarks!" he said. "I really don't know what to do with him!"

"Or without him!" she added, smiling.

"Indeed not! He's invaluable." He returned her smile, with that little glint in his eyes, which at the moment seemed entirely kindly.

"I hope, Miss Minster, that you won't take against our part of the country through your misadventure?" Mr. Kirby enquired, thereby drawing her attention to himself and away from Sir Richard.

She made a diplomatically evasive reply by saying that no doubt the area would appear more kindly in the summer, which he assured her was true, going on to enthuse about the quality of the sport available in the district, as killing various forms of wild-life seemed to be his main interest, and it did not seem to occur to him that Miss

Minster might not find these activities equally fascinating. She listened with polite attention, and managed to slip in a question of her own, asking if by any chance he was acquainted with the Partridges. He replied that he knew Sir Marmaduke slightly, but then went on to enthuse about a hunt in which he had recently participated, in the course of which most of the field and several couple of hounds seemed to have met with disaster in one form or another. Sir Richard had no difficulty in recalling her interest to himself by remarking that it might be as well to think of adjourning to the chapel across the road if they were not to be late for the service. He did not mention that, when Miss Minster mentioned the name "Partridge," Mr. Tupper had looked at her with a little frown, and had shaken his head and tut-tutted in a concerned manner.

Miss Minster excused herself and went upstairs to put on her bonnet, redingote and cloak, followed by Mr. Kirby, who took the opportunity to say to her as he ascended at her heels, "I must say I'm very glad you are here, or Christmas would be very dull indeed in this lonely place!"

Flattered by the implied compliment, Miss Minster turned at the head of the stairs to make a suitably modest reply, and was disconcerted and embarrassed to find the handsome young man gazing up at her with an alarmingly ardent expression of admiration, so that she answered him more shortly than she intended, and hastened to her room, scrambling into her outdoor clothing in order to be returned downstairs before he emerged from his own room. She found Sir Richard in the entrance hall, being helped into his helmet and redingote by Jem, who had brought them down to save him climbing the stairs, it being an awkward and painful business for him.

"Art fit, lass?" Sir Richard enquired, with a parody of a northern accent, accompanied by his infectious smile, which she could not help but return.

"Should we not wait for Mr. Kirby?" she enquired.

"Oh, he'll catch up—I can't go at a trot, you know!" he replied lightly, offering her his arm. She took it, and was glad of its support as they crossed the road and climbed the short slope to the chapel, for the cleared path had a number of treacherously icy patches. Jem plodded behind, humming a Christmas carol to himself, and Mr. Kirby caught them up as they entered the little stone building.

CHAPTER FIVE

THE CHAPEL WAS not unlike a barn inside, with white-washed walls, a few small windows, a table covered with a white cloth against the east wall, a simple wooden lectern, and benches for seating. About twenty people were already assembled, not counting the dozen or so sheep-dogs who lurked behind their master's legs, or, in one case, sat beside him on a bench, studiously ignoring each other. Mine host of the Nag's Head and his wife were in the front row, and she turned to beckon the newcomers to join them. Miss Minster, Sir Richard and Mr. Kirby made their way to her down the narrow central aisle, being well stared at on the way, and found that there was just room for them on the front bench, Miss Minster in the middle, with a gentleman on either side. Jem slipped in beside the maids from the inn, halfway down the aisle, and they obligingly shifted up to make room for him, with a great deal in the way of grinning and flirtatious glances.

A gnarled old man with a full white beard, who might have passed for Elijah had he not been dressed in neat cord breeches and a homespun coat, read his way through the service, standing at the lectern. Miss Minster found the familiar words easy enough to follow, despite his broad speech, and it was a moving experience to join in the dignified service, with the small congregation reciting the responses with simple fervour, and to hear the gospel for Christmas Day being read by a real shepherd, leaning on his crook. His dog went to the front with him, and sat gazing up into his face as he read.

When the prayers began, Miss Minster sank to her knees on the stone floor without hesitation, and Sir Richard, forgetting his knee, attempted to join her, stuck halfway, and had the mortification of being heaved back on to his seat by the landlady, while the man reading the service waited patiently for him to be settled. Mr. Kirby took one look at the stone flags, and remained seated.

The congregation chanted the psalms unaccompanied, and sang "Oh Come, All Ye Faithful" to a fiddle played by the shepherd who had read the lesson. During this, the collection was taken up. Miss Minster put two of her precious shillings in the almsbag, and caught a glimpse of gold as Sir Richard dropped in his offering—more than one coin, too, judging by the clink as they reached the bottom.

After the service, the churchwarden came to speak to the visitors, so they were almost the last to leave the building. They paused outside to look about them at what had become a very beautiful scene, for the sun was shining brightly, the snow was dazzlingly white, and the stream which leapt down the fellside in a series of little cascades, to plunge under the road and run down to the lake, was festooned with icicles hanging from the rocky ledges and the little sallows which clung precariously to its banks. The ridge beyond the lake still looked like a giant's bolster in a clean linen cover, and a variety of wildfowl slithered about on the ice of the lake. Even the stark black trees were transformed with a trimming of snow and ice.

"The lake looks good for skating," Mr. Kirby remarked. "I wonder if there are any skates at the inn. Do you care for the sport?" he asked, turning to Miss Minster.

"I've never tried," she replied. "Not having lived near enough to a suitable stretch of water."

"I used to..." Sir Richard said quietly, more to himself than his companions, then sighed.

They began to walk slowly back towards the inn, and then Mr. Kirby asked if they minded if he hurried on ahead to see what effect Jem's poultice had achieved.

"I thought the river sometimes froze at Maidstone?" Sir Richard remarked.

"Yes, it does, but I've only lived there while I was governessing, and learning to skate was out of the question then."

"Ain't governesses allowed any pleasures?"

"Very few. I suppose we are expected to be so enraptured by the achievements of our pupils that we don't require any other excitement!"

"Sounds remarkably dull." Sir Richard hesitated, and then said slowly, prodding the ground with his stick and apparently studying the result with close attention, "Look here, Dorcas, we may consider ourselves friends, may we not—after being well-nigh lost in the snow together?"

"Is it possible for two people of such differing social classes to be friends?" she demurred.

"How, different? I'm a baronet, and you're the daughter of another."

"I was, but now I'm merely a governess, and if anyone cares to think of me as anyone's daughter, it can only be of a gambler, a drunkard, a bankrupt, and a suicide." She spoke bitterly and turned her face away from him. Perhaps the sun or the cold wind made her eyes water.

Sir Richard gave a particularly vicious prod with his stick and said gruffly, "That ain't as I choose to think of you. You were very much a friend to me when I was in need of help, and I'd like to be as much as you. To put it shortly, or we'll freeze to death before I get to the point, will you let me give you some blunt to tide you over?''

"You're very kind," she said, turning her sad grey eyes on him with a look of wonder. "But it would be most improper, and I really couldn't accept."

"Well, at least you didn't fly into alt at the idea. You'll let me lend you something, then."

"I don't know what to do," she murmured, looking and sounding so unhappy that Sir Richard took a step towards her, recollected himself, and retired the same distance.

"Well, I'll not try to force you, but...I know! Ask old Tupper! I'll wager you three guineas to a kiss that he'll advise you to accept!"

"I thought you didn't gamble?" Miss Minster replied with a little smile, assuming that he was joking. They had reached the road by now, and as they stepped across it to the door of the Nag's Head, she added in a low, nervous voice, "You're very kind indeed, and as I am sure I shall not be able to pay my bill here, may I ask you to lend me the difference until June?"

"But that will leave you with nothing!"

"I shall manage," she replied grimly, having had to "manage" several times in the past few years.

Sir Richard let the matter drop for the moment, having made a little more progress in his campaign, and said, "I wish I could teach you to skate. I used to be quite good at it, but that's gone now, along with my colours."

"Shall you mind very much, having to leave the Army?"

He sighed. "Not really. I only joined because m'father expected it. I've no room for complaint—I'm still alive, and not lost the leg or anything vital, like some poor fellows I know. I'll have plenty to do, managing my estates.

I'm adding to them quite considerably, and I'll have a little gig and drive around, keeping my eye on things and talking turnips and pigs with m'tenants, like old Coke at Holkham. I'll go to London sometimes, to see m'friends, and I've plenty of books. I dare say I shall find a wife, and have children to look to. It don't sound too bad at all, do it?"

"It sounds idyllic!" Miss Minster replied sincerely, for it was just such a life as she would have chosen for herself.

As they entered the inn, there was much sound of activity in the back regions, but no-one was about in the hall. Sir Richard eyed the kissing-bunch as Miss Minster removed her bonnet, and said, "Er—Miss Minster?"

"Yes?"

He advanced to a suitable position, and said, "Would you mind coming here a moment?"

She walked over to him, looking enquiring and a trifle puzzled. He flicked a glance upwards, and she followed it and saw the kissing-bunch a fraction too late, for he took her by the shoulders and gently kissed her lips.

"Happy Christmas, m'dear!"

"And very nice too!" said a sardonic voice from the doorway of the tap-room, where Mr. Black was lounging against the frame, hands thrust into the flap of his drab breeches and his coat hooked back by his arms to display a distressingly vulgar purple brocaded waistcoat. "Any to spare?"

"I only kiss pretty ladies," Sir Richard replied equably, "And I don't place you in that category."

Mr. Black gave a bark of laughter. "Very good! Well, I ain't one for trespassing!" he said, and retired into the tap-room.

"Odious man!" Miss Minster said indignantly. Sir Richard thought she meant himself for a moment, but her glare was directed at the tap-room door, so he took heart and followed her into the dining-room, where Mr. Tupper was found seated at the table with his papers spread out in neat little piles. He looked at them over his spectacles and enquired if they had enjoyed the service.

"Very much," Sir Richard replied, going to kick the logs in the fireplace into greater activity. "Mr. Tupper, may we trespass on your time and expertise for a moment?"

Mr. Tupper gave him a suspicious look and replied cautiously that they might.

"The matter is, that Miss Minster finds herself a trifle short of the ready, through the unexpected expense of being delayed on her journey. I've offered to lend her a little to help her out, but she's naturally doubtful about entering into such an arrangement with a comparative stranger. How would you advise her, as a knowledgeable and responsible sort of man?"

"Oh, I would never advise anyone to get into debt!" Mr. Tupper replied at once. " 'Neither a lender nor a borrower be', you know! No, I wouldn't advise that at all!"

Miss Minster bit her lip, partly from anxiety about her financial situation, and partly to stop herself from correcting his misquotation. She was glad afterwards that she had said nothing, for he went on, leaning back in his chair and placing his fingers together in a proper judicial manner, "Of course, that will not solve the young lady's difficulty. I think I may say, however, that a solution occurs to me. I propose, Sir Richard, that, if you are agreeable, you and I might contrive between us to—er—to 'pay the shot', I think you would term it, eh, Sir?"

Sir Richard intimated that he might employ such a phrase, and that the idea seemed to him a very good one. Miss Minster's attempts to protest and to thank them were completely drowned out by the entry of Jem with a heavy tray loaded with steaming tankards, which he set down with a crash on the table. He was closely attended by the cat Maurice, which sat itself discreetly in the safe area between Sir Richard's feet and blinked inscrutably at the world, or as much of it as he could see through a forest of table- and chair-legs.

"'Ot Tiger!" Jem announced. "Just the thing ter stop yer froat freezing!"

He had Sir Richard out of his redingote and took his helmet in a twinkling, collected Miss Minster's bonnet, coat and cloak, scooped up the cat, which muttered indignantly, and bore the lot away, while Mr. Tupper handed Miss Minster one of the smaller tankards. She peered into it rather dubiously, for, although it held only half a pint, it was full of amber liquid which smelled very spicy and flavoursome.

"What is it?" she enquired.

"Good stuff for cold weather," Sir Richard assured her. "Only spiced and mulled ale . . ." He paused and did not go on until she had tasted, found it pleasant, and taken a couple of mouthfuls " . . . half and half with sherry!" he finished rapidly. She choked slightly as some went down the wrong way, but recovered and gamely drank most of her tankard-full, for it was very good and warming.

Mr. Petts entered silently and buried his lantern-jaw in one of the larger tankards. "Cold out," he volunteered when he emerged again, to which the others could only agree.

One of the maids came in to spread the cloth on the table, so Mr. Tupper had to collect up his papers. Under cover of the flurry, Sir Richard went over to Miss Minster, took her hand, and dropped three golden guineas into it. "Lost m'wager," he said happily. "Serves me right, but I thought Mr. Tupper'ld come down on my side!"

"You thought nothing of the kind!" she replied in a sharp whisper. Their eyes met, and hers dropped first, for that odd little gleam was back in his, and it made her feel distinctly short of breath, and even a little afraid.

"I think you're a very wilful man," she said unsteadily, "and more than a little unscrupulous!"

"Oh, come! I'm very scrupulous!" he protested. "Scrupulous to a fault! I never go to bed in m'boots, or cheat at penny-brag! In fact, I never even *play* penny-brag!"

"Ah, grub at last!" Mr. Black exclaimed, flinging open the door and striding in with unnecessary vigour, then, seeing that so far only the cloth had been laid and nothing edible had appeared on it, "'Ere, we ain't dining with Duke 'Umphrey, I 'opes? Ain't these clumpertons got the prog ready yet?"

"It's barely noon," Mr. Tupper said severely, "And would you please speak more quietly! There's no need to shout!"

Mr. Black sniffed, gave him a sidelong look, and sat down at the table. When the maids and Jem brought in the dishes, he lifted the covers and helped himself without waiting for the others.

Mr. Kirby hurried in, apologising for his lateness, and expressed himself delighted and amazed by the improvement in his mare's condition. He darted forward to hold Miss Minster's chair, but was neatly forestalled by Sir Richard, who murmured, "I fear Black's a mite elevated," in her ear as she sat down. Mr. Kirby took the place on her right again, and gave her a spirited and detailed account of his mare's life history, which was fortunately not overlong, as she was a three-year-old.

If Mr. Black was drunk, he soon sobered once he had taken the edge off his appetite, so perhaps he was only irritated by a fancied lateness in the arrival of luncheon. He embarked presently on what he seemed to intend as pleasant conversation.

"Don't often find a gentry-cove travelling in a common cross-mail," he said to Sir Richard. "Officers usually 'as their own drag, or 'ires a yellow-bounder."

"My coach broke a wheel, which couldn't be repaired in time," Sir Richard replied. "And there wasn't a post chaise to be had."

"Oh," Mr. Black lost interest. "I knows about you," he said to Mr. Tupper. "You're a puzzle-cove, but what about you, Miss?"

"I'm a governess," Miss Minster replied chillingly, sounding exactly like one, at which he pulled a face, sniffed, and turned to Mr. Petts. "What d'you do, cully?"

Mr. Petts regarded him with a marked lack of expression, and replied with unusual humour, "Well, as you're a prig-napper, I don't mind owning to being a padborrower."

"And pray, what is that?" Miss Minster enquired.

"A horse-thief!" Sir Richard told her, laughing, but he caught Mr. Petts's eye and they exchanged a look which, for some reason, made Sir Richard change the subject by remarking how good the food was at the Nag's Head, which drew warm agreement from the others, even Mr. Black, for the landlady's idea of a light luncheon consisted of generous slices of cold beef, mutton and ham, potatoes roasted in their jackets, three large jars of pick-

les, a sizeable cheese, a loaf and a crock of butter, and a
fruit cake.

Jem came in with various pots of ale and a pot of tea,
and said to his master in an anxious undertone, "'Ere, sir!
Is your place in 'Ampshire worf more'n a 'undred a
year?"

"I should hope so!" replied Sir Richard. "Why do you
ask?"

"Covess was wondering if you'd go aht termorrer and
shoot a few birds and fings. Says you might be qualified,
bein' a landowner, like. Don't know what she means,
meself."

"Your man must be a townee!" Mr. Tupper remarked. "The landlady is referring to the Game Act of
1671, which limited the taking of game to a small number of categories of persons, one such being the owner of
land worth more than one hundred pounds per annum.
Sterling," he added, lest they should suspect he meant
Scots, or jam.

"Oh—yes, of course!" Sir Richard was enlightened.
"Ain't there any poachers about here, then?"

"The magistrates about here enforce the Game Laws
very strictly, and apply the maximum fines and terms of
imprisonment allowed by the various amendments to the
law," Mr. Tupper informed him. "So, you see, one can
hardly blame our hostess for seizing an opportunity to—
er—supplement her larder by legitimate means!"

"But my land's in Hampshire, not Cumberland!" Sir
Richard objected.

"That makes no difference." Mr. Tupper was enjoying
this opportunity to instruct his betters. "Game is wild and
cannot be private property while it is alive, so a qualified
person may take it anywhere in the kingdom, on any land,

unless he has been specifically warned-off a particular property by its owner or his servant beforehand."

"There y'are!" said Jem, who had been listening to all this with great interest. "So you can go aht in the morning and shoot the covess a few grice and rabbits."

"Grice?" queried Sir Richard, appalled.

"Grouses?" Jem offered hopefully.

"Tell her that I'll be delighted to shoot her some grouse, or whatever, if I can come near them, but I can't walk far in this snow."

"Easy as—er—falling aht o' bed!" Jem replied, restraining himself in deference to Miss Minster. "We'll 'arness up the sledge and go in comfort, put a bit o' corn abaht, and there y'are!"

"I shudder to think what the Beau would say!" Sir Richard murmured, putting his hand over his eyes for a moment, "Shooting sitting grice—grouse and out of season, at that!"

"Is the Marquess a sportsman, then?" Miss Minster could not resist demonstrating that she—now—knew whom he meant by "the Beau."

"He's very fond of a pheasant shoot, 'though he's a remarkably poor shot—generally peppers the keepers more than the birds! He keeps his own pack of hounds in the Peninsula, for hunting in the winter, when it's the close season for fighting."

"I'll flap me 'ands and make 'em fly a bit," Jem offered soothingly.

"Oh, very well! I suppose it's the least I can do, when we've been so very well looked after," Sir Richard replied. "'Though I don't much care for shooting things."

"Apart from Frenchmen," Mr. Kirby observed smilingly.

"Not even them," Sir Richard replied seriously. "I've not been a soldier from choice, but because m'father wished it."

Mr. Kirby, no doubt feeling that his jovial remark had fallen flat, redeemed himself by saying, "I'll come with you, if I may. I'm qualified too, as a landowner, and I have my guns with me. It'll help pass the time while we wait for the thaw."

When they had finished their collation, Mr. Black went off to "see to 'is 'orse," he said, and the others adjourned to the parlour, where Mr. Tupper made himself comfortable before the fire and indulged in a little nap. Mr. Petts extended himself along the settle with the book he had borrowed, and showed signs of following suit. Sir Richard sat by his little table and put his leg on the stool, Miss Minster sat opposite him, and Mr. Kirby fidgetted about for a while, and then excused himself, saying he would have a word or two with Jem about his mare, and some other horses he owned, adding, "I'll not be long" with a smile for Miss Minster, as if this important news was intended to comfort her.

"What makes you think Black ain't a thief-taker?" Sir Richard asked Mr. Petts.

"I didn't say that," he evaded.

"You implied it."

Mr. Petts sniffed and rubbed the side of his nose reflectively. "'E may be a thief-taker, but 'e ain't a Robin Redbreast."

"How do you know?"

Mr. Petts winked, and tapped his nose with his finger. "I knows 'ow a Runner be'aves, and 'e ain't right! O' course, 'e maybe said that just to make 'imself sound more important." With that, he closed his eyes and apparently fell asleep.

"Do you think Mr. Petts is right?" Miss Minster asked.

Sir Richard shrugged. "Can't say, m'dear, never having encountered a Bow Street Runner m'self, so I'd not know what to expect. I don't much like Black, I'll admit."

After a moment's silence, Miss Minster took his three guineas from her reticule, placed them on the table in a small, neat pile, and pushed them over to him.

"I've no wish to appear ungrateful," she said quietly, "For I am, indeed, very grateful to you, but I cannot take this money."

"Why not? You won it in a fair wager."

"I did not accept the wager, for I never do . . . you understand . . . In any case, it was not fair, because you knew very well that no responsible lawyer would ever advise anyone in my position to borrow money! You offered the wager with every intention of losing it!"

"I'd rather have won, for you'd still have had the money, and I'd have won the prize! Have it as a loan, then."

Miss Minster felt an odd, excited tremor as she understood the meaning of his first sentence, but thought it best to avoid his gaze and ignore it. "Please don't press me!" she said in some agitation. "I'll accept Mr. Tupper's kind suggestion if I need to do so, and I shall pay back whatever I borrow in June, if that will be convenient."

"Plenty of time to consider that later," he replied. "I'll be at m'sister's for a few weeks, and I'll call on you at the Partridges', if you'll permit me. To see if you're happily settled, you know."

Miss Minster hesitated overlong and looked distressed and anxious. "It's very kind of you to think of it, but I doubt if my employer will allow me to receive a caller."

"I'll bring m'sister. She can be the caller, and I'll accompany her. He couldn't possibly object to that!"

"I didn't just mean a gentleman caller. A governess is only a superior servant, you see, and it wouldn't be at all the thing for me to expect to be allowed *any* callers. I'm sorry." There was a real note of regret in her voice, which she heard with surprise and misgiving, thinking herself very foolish to be so happy that he had offered, and so wretched to know it was impossible.

"Hmm," Sir Richard sounded unconvinced. "It might be a good thing for them to know you've friends of consequence in the district. M'goodbrother's a magistrate. I'll try, anyway, and I may write to you, at least?"

"I—I suppose so..." Miss Minster's spirits gave a sudden lift.

"Only if you'd like it."

She gave a shy, uncertain smile. "I'd like it very much." Then, afraid she had sounded too eager, "I don't get any letters."

"I'll have 'em franked, so you needn't fear the postage. D'you know, it cost m'sister a *shilling* to receive a letter I wrote her from London? Downright robbery! I think perhaps I'll go into Parliament and have my own franks!"

Miss Minster could not help laughing at the thought of anyone going to the trouble and expense of entering Parliament merely in order to have the privilege of sending letters that the recipients need not pay to receive.

"That's better!" he said approvingly. "Now you're more cheerful. You've been looking quite blue-devilled today, and it won't do at Christmas! You've no need to worry about your bill here, and you're saved from the Partridges for a little longer, and you've a very handsome fellow paying you attention, so what more could you wish?''

Miss Minster's smile faded, and she said in a quiet, thoughtful tone, ''It is pleasant to be reprieved for a few more days, for I cannot help worrying about my future. I know nothing about the Partridges, and it is so easy for someone in my position to be made wretched by an unsympathetic employer. And this country is so harsh and wild! I had not realised it would be like this! I feel helpless, and far from everything familiar, 'though that's foolish, for I'm no more alone in the world than I was in Kent, but at least there, the scenes around me were familiar, even if there was no-one to turn to, but here I feel lost...'' She sought her handkerchief in her reticule, and resolutely dabbed her eyes.

''I bet you'll feel you can turn to me!'' Sir Richard said with a fierce scowl. ''If you don't like the Partridges, or you ain't happy, write and tell me, and at least I'll help you find a better place!''

''You're very kind...''

He made an impatient movement with his shoulders and said abruptly, ''The fire wants mending!'' There was a fractional pause as he made to get up, then realised that he would have to kneel before the hearth, which he could not manage with any dignity.

''I'll do it!'' Miss Minster said quickly, and busied herself placing several logs from the basket standing by the hearth among the glowing embers which were all that was left of the fire. It took a few minutes to ensure that they would catch and burn properly, and it gave her time to recover her composure. Sir Richard employed the time in picking up the three guineas and the reticule which she had left on the table, and pushing the coins right down to the bottom of it. By the time she returned to her seat, the reticule was lying closed, as she had left it, and he was sorting out the dominoes.

Mr. Kirby returned just as they were beginning a game of thumpers, and proposed himself as a third party, drawing up a chair a little too close to Miss Minster's, and indulging in a little flirtation with her as they played, thereby paying the penalty of inattention and being soundly beaten several times in succession by Sir Richard, who seemed suddenly to have fallen into a mild attack of the blue devils himself.

After an hour or so of this harmless occupation, Mr. Kirby became restless and proposed a short walk before dark, for he said being indoors all day made him stuffy, and the wind had cleared the road of much of its burden of snow. The other two players were agreeable, and went out to the hall, where Sir Richard called Jem and sent him for their outdoor clothing.

A few minutes later, they set off along the road which ran beside the lake. The wind had undoubtedly changed very much for the better, being fully southwest by now, and the snow was slowly beginning to melt. Progress on the road was not too difficult for Miss Minster and Mr. Kirby, but Sir Richard, after limping along gamely for a quarter mile, said irritably that he thought he would turn back.

Miss Minster, whose attention had been taken up by Mr. Kirby's chatter, turned to look at him in concern.

"Oh, how thoughtless of us! We've been going too fast for you, I'm afraid! Yes, of course we'll go back."

"No need for you to do that," Sir Richard replied. "You go on—it will do you good. I'll stroll back at my own pace."

Mr. Kirby was also anxious for her to continue, so Miss Minster reluctantly continued walking, looking back once or twice to see if Sir Richard was managing. Despite Mr. Kirby's undoubted charm and good looks, and his pleasantly attentive manner towards her, she had an alarmingly strong feeling that she would rather have stayed with Sir Richard, which was odd, because Mr. Kirby behaved very correctly, even in his flirtatious moments, whereas Sir Richard had certainly behaved quite outrageously once or twice. She thought of his successful trickery in catching her under the kissing-bunch that morning, and felt her colour rise at the thought of it, and of her own lack of resistance or remonstrance.

"The cold has given you a very becoming touch of colour!" Mr. Kirby declared with satisfaction. "If I may say so, Miss Minster, you're a very pretty young lady. I consider myself very fortunate to have been snowed up here with you!"

Miss Minster smiled a little at his flattery, and turned it aside by enquiring, "In spite of the accident to your poor horse?"

"Oh, that—well, that does rather spoil it," he admitted, disconcerted. "But that peculiar fellow of Sir Richard's seems to know what he's about, and has her able to put her foot to the ground already. I was afraid she'd go on three legs after such a twist! Actually, I was talking to him after luncheon, and offered him a place in my stables, but he wouldn't hear of it, even when I offered to go well above what Severall pays him! He said it wasn't a matter of money, which seemed to me very odd!"

"I think he is very attached to his master," Miss Minster replied. "They have gone through some difficult times together, and have saved one another's life on occasion, so there must be a strong bond between them."

"Oh? Ah, well, I suppose that's why Severall puts up with his peculiar behaviour!" Mr. Kirby rambled on at some length about his own servants and estate, until they had walked the best part of a mile from the inn, and the sun had dropped behind the western fells.

"It is growing dark and cold," Miss Minster pointed out, when her companion's flow of talk ceased for a moment. "I think we should turn about now."

Mr. Kirby agreed at once, and they retraced their steps in the winter dusk, Mr. Kirby continuing to talk about his own interests. Near the point where they had parted from Sir Richard, Miss Minster stumbled, and Mr. Kirby put a hand on her waist to steady her, but did not remove it when she had recovered her balance. When she tried to move a little away from him in a natural manner, the hand slid round further and drew her back again, and she was just trying to think of some way of disengaging herself without giving offence or putting herself to the embarrassment of saying anything about it, when Sir Richard stepped out from a group of trees by the roadside and said, "Ah, there you are! I was beginning to wonder if you'd been carried off by wolves!"

Mr. Kirby's hand unobtrusively removed itself, and Miss Minster contrived to put Sir Richard between them, and said a little breathlessly, "I'm sure you would have heard some disturbance if that had been the case!"

"Should you have screamed?" Sir Richard asked with apparent interest.

"Oh, very loudly!"

"And, of course, the wolves would have made some sort of unpleasant sound as they gobbled you up!"

"There ain't any wolves in England," Mr. Kirby said prosaically, sounding puzzled.

"Ain't there?" replied Sir Richard. "You should look very carefully at what's inside all these sheepskins walking about on the fells, you know—you might get quite a surprise!"

CHAPTER SIX

WHEN THEY RETURNED to the parlour at the Nag's Head, they found Mr. Tupper and Mr. Petts snoring gently, but one of the maids brought in the teatray, and the resulting clatter of cups and dishes woke them.

"Dear me!" said Mr. Tupper. "I meant to take a little stroll this afternoon, but I see it's dark already!"

Mr. Petts said nothing, but went to hand cups in the proper drawing-room manner as Miss Minster poured the tea. The cat Maurice had insinuated himself into the room under cover of the maid's skirts, and sat squarely in front of Sir Richard, staring him in the face, until he enquired politely if the animal would like some milk. Apparently, this was the right question, for the cat purred loudly and lapped elegantly at the quantity which Sir Richard poured into a dish from the large jugful provided, and placed under the table for the cat's convenience. After that, it jumped into its benefactor's lap and settled down for a session of stroking and scratching behind the ears.

"He seems to have taken a great fancy to you," Miss Minster observed.

"Yes. Animals often do," he replied in tones of mild surprise. "I expect they know I like 'em. Mind you, it can be embarrassing at times, if the creature belongs to someone else! One of the Beau's foxhounds took to following me about last winter, and every time I looked round, there he was with his nose to m'boot, waving his stern and looking at me with eyes like twopenny pieces, as if he expected me to be about to give him a dozen foxes in aspic! The Beau looked down his beak at me something alarming! Probably thought I meant to steal the beast!''

"He has quite an imposing beak, I believe,'' Miss Minster recalled the dominant feature of some cartoons she had seen of the noble Marquess.

"Yes, the men call him Nosey, or Out Atty. Not that it's grotesque, or anything. In fact, he's quite a handsome man, and very popular with the ladies—but the nose is strong and aquiline, and he has a way of arching his eyebrows and holding his head *so*, and saying something in that abrupt way of his, very short and to the point... He's four inches shorter than I, but he reduces me to a dwarf with one look! One can't help liking him, though, for he's scrupulously fair and treats everyone the same, and he knows what he's doing, which is more than you can say for some generals! There was never an army as well-fed and looked-after as Our Atty's, and he makes the medical corps keep up instead of lagging three days behind, which is why I still have two legs to m'name! I hope he gets to Paris before the Tsar and Schwarzenburg—he deserves it!''

"And yet the Russians have done very well,'' Miss Minster observed fairly.

"Oh, yes, I'll not deny it! But there are millions of them, and the Beau has never had above eighty thousand, including the Portuguese. A hundred thousand, if you count the Spanish, but they're so unreliable. Brave enough, but half-starved and with no more sense and discipline than a flock of starlings! They think if you say Tuesday, Saturday or Monday will do as well!'' He caught sight of Mr. Kirby's face, looking singularly *ennuyé*, and broke off with an apologetic, "I'm sorry—I run on too much. I must be boring you," to Miss Minster.

"Not at all. It's very interesting. You have a great deal to remember."

"Yes." Sir Richard absent-mindedly scratched the cat's head with one gentle finger as it presented particularly itchy places to his attention, "And I've plenty to look forward to, as well, when I can get about more. I'll have horses and dogs and cats, cattle, sheep, pigs, and I think a couple of donkeys. I like to see a donkey or two about the place. The children could ride them—if I have any, that is." He unconsciously rubbed his injured knee, and Miss Minster recalled what he had said about females not wishing to marry a cripple. She wished there was some way of conveying to him that he was wrong, for she was quite certain that she would not be deterred...

She suddenly realised where her thoughts were leading her, and busied herself offering everyone a second cup of tea. Mr. Kirby seized the opportunity to break in on Sir Richard's monopoly of her attention, and engage her in conversation himself, apparently not noticing that her response was distinctly cool, for she had not at all liked his attempt to put his arm round her. Sir Richard, who could see quite well in the dark, did notice it, and concealed his amusement by concentrating his attention on the area under the cat's chin.

Jem came in to collect the tray, and caught sight of the animal. "'Ere!" he exclaimed, "I told yer before you ain't supposed to sit with the Quality! You're a below-stairs cully, you are! You didn't ought to let 'im sit on yer sir! 'E'll 'ave spread 'is 'ackles all over yer Inexpressibles, and a regiment o' Light Bobs as well, I shouldn't wonder!"

"I think not," replied Sir Richard. "He's a very clean person," but he allowed Jem to remove the cat, which seemed to like Jem even more than his master, and went off with him, muffler-fashion as before, after failing in an attempt to get inside Jem's coat.

"Dinner in an *h*our!" Jem warned them as he left.

Mr. Tupper pulled out his watch and declared that he would go and change in fifteen minutes. Miss Minster, intending to make an extra effort with her appearance in honour of the day, made her excuses and left the gentlemen.

At the foot of the stairs, she encountered Mr. Black on his way down. He halted on the bottom step, blocking her progress, his unpleasant smile looking particularly saturnine in the dim light produced by the branch of candles on the hall table.

"Orf to make yourself look pretty, then?" he asked.

"I'm going to change for dinner," she replied.

"What you want is a bright silk, with a bit o' bosom showing," he informed her. "Let your 'air down and frizz it a bit, and put a string o' sparklers round your neck. You'd look quite the flash mort, I reckon."

"If you would kindly let me pass," she said coldly.

"'Ow about a kiss under the mistletoe?" he suggested.

"What d'you charge for a pint of claret?" Sir Richard enquired from the dining-room doorway. His tone was mild and pleasant, but that little thread of steel was clearly apparent below the surface.

Mr. Black stepped down from the stairs and sidled across the hall.

"I don't mill with a badger-leg," he replied. "Anyway, I was only passing a few pleasantries. No need to cut up over that! I don't want your laced-mutton—she ain't my style," and with that, he vanished into the taproom.

"Damned impudence!" Sir Richard remarked calmly.

"Would you mind translating that exchange into English?" Miss Minster requested, her annoyance with Mr. Black giving her voice a touch of asperity.

"Mr. Black suggested that you might appear quite the lady, of a certain kind, if you dressed the part. I offered to punch him on the nose, but he declined the honour on the grounds that he don't wish to fight a cripple, and added his assurance that he has no particular designs on your virtue."

"Oh," Miss Minster thoughtfully checked this version against what she could recall of the cant, and then enquired, "And a 'laced-mutton'?"

"I'd rather not say. It ain't a proper way to describe a lady."

"I suppose it's the inevitable result of travelling without a chaperon," she sighed, starting to climb the stairs. Sir Richard, who suspected that it was as much the result of Black's having seen him kiss her that morning, and therefore his fault, followed her in his halting fashion in silence.

"He need not have been so rude to you," she went on. "Why 'badger-leg'?"

"Badgers are supposed to have legs of differing lengths."

"Are they? You mean, each of the four is different? How odd! Is it true?"

"Can't say. I've never been sufficiently intimate with a badger to offer to measure his legs."

Miss Minster's imagination presented her with a picture of Sir Richard in close conversation with a badger, which looked like a furry version of Mr. Tupper, and she began to laugh, coming to a stop as she did so. Sir Richard bumped into her.

"You ain't crying, are you?" he asked anxiously.

"No, laughing," she replied, and tried to explain. Having a lively imagination himself, he caught the picture exactly, and laughed with her.

"And if I asked to measure his legs, he'd say 'I really would not advise you to try, my dear sir!'" he gasped, and threw them into a further paroxysm.

Miss Minster was still laughing as she went into her own room. The fire was burning brightly, and when she had lit the candles, it looked very cosy and welcoming. She took down the gown which she had put out that morning and looked it over. The creases had disappeared and it was perfectly wearable.

There was a soft tapping at the door, and she laid the dress across the bed and went to see who it was.

"I—er—" began Sir Richard, who was standing outside the door when she opened it. "I've a little Christmas gift for you—nothing much, just a token." He thrust a tissue-wrapped package into her hands.

"Oh! But I couldn't . . . I've nothing to give you in exchange, and, besides, it's not at all proper . . ."

"Oh, fiddlesticks! Who's to know? I don't want anything in exchange. It's only a pretty gewgaw. To tell truth, it's one of the trifles I brought m'sister from Spain, but I've plenty of others for her, and she wouldn't grudge you it."

"You—you're very kind," Miss Minster said in a low, tremulous voice. She was looking down at the package in her hands and trying to recall the last time anyone had given her a present. It seemed a very long time ago.

Sir Richard stepped forward as if impelled by some outside force, dropped his stick, cupped her head in his right hand, slid his left arm about her waist, drew her close, and as she looked up in surprise, bent to kiss her full on the lips.

Up to this point in her life, Miss Minster had always assumed that a kiss was effected by one person pressing his or her lips against those of another person. She was considerably startled and shaken to discover in the next few minutes that there was far more to it than that, and the effects were extremely far-reaching and shattering, involving every nerve and fibre of her body. She felt quite faint. Sir Richard was obviously considerably more experienced, for he retained sufficient presence of mind to remove all her hairpins with his right hand while he was kissing her.

Eventually, his lips reluctantly parted from hers, and he raised his head. She stood quite still for a second, as if she were stunned, and then she stepped back sharply, breaking out of the circle of his arm, shut the door of her room in his face, and leaned against it with her eyes closed until her heart slowed to a more normal beat, and then she stumbled across to the bed and sat down on the edge of it.

"Oh, how could he? And I let him . . . !" Then she recollected that he had kissed her twice before, and she had not objected, so how could he be blamed for assuming . . . whatever it was that he had assumed! Tears filled her eyes, brimmed over and rolled down her cheeks, and she let them fall, crying soundlessly and hopelessly.

After some minutes, she gave herself a shake and murmured, "Come now, stop this at once! It's entirely your own fault! Oh, but he is so kind, and I thought he understood . . ." To stop herself from weeping again, she adopted a sharp, brittle tone and went on, "Well now, what does he consider a suitable gewgaw for a—a 'laced-mutton'?" and angrily pulled at the blue ribbon tied round the package and ripped off the tissue-paper.

It was a shawl. A black silk Spanish shawl thickly embroidered with exotic flowers in softly-coloured silks and edged with a long knotted fringe. She sat staring at it, and gradually the feeling of desolation and anger faded, and she was left with a curious mixture of uncertainty and excitement which made her quite breathless.

"It's very lovely. He must have meant it kindly, surely?"

Draping it round her shoulders, she went to look in the mirror, which was too small to show the full splendour of it, but the soft touch of the silk against her neck was comforting, and for some reason made her feel less alone in the world. She found herself thinking, in a muddled, half-reluctant way, that he was very kind, and being kissed by him was not at all unpleasant . . .

"I'll be persuading myself to let him do *anything* in a moment!" she said aloud, and, casting the shawl aside, unbuttoned her daydress and pulled it off, poured cold water in the bowl, and washed her face briskly to remove the traces of tears, adopting an attitude of angry defiance, a determination not to allow herself to appear disturbed in any way by Sir Richard's dreadful behaviour.

Her evening gown was a fine sky-blue velvet, a trifle straighter in the skirts, and perhaps an inch lower in the waist than the present mode, with long, tight sleeves fastened at the wrist with little silver buttons, and a narrow edging of swansdown round the low neckline.

Fastening the wrist-buttons, she crossed to the tallboy and tilted the mirror in an attempt to see as much of herself as she could. The gown looked quite well, but she was thinner than she had been when it was new, and it hung a trifle loose. The low neck left a very bare expanse of skin, but she took a string of little glass beads from her trunk— a cheap, tawdry thing which had not been considered worth selling with the rest of her modest collection of jewellery towards the settlement of her father's debts. It added a touch of colour and sparkle in the candlelight.

It was only now that she realised that her hair was down about her shoulders, although she must have pushed it aside unknowingly when she washed. She stared at her reflection in astonishment, unable to understand how this could have happened, and then realised that Sir Richard must have unpinned it, and, moreover, made off with her hairpins! She went to look in her trunk for some more, but caught sight of the ribbon from his gift, lying on the floor where she had flung it. It was a very good match with her gown.

After a momentary hesitation, she picked it up and smoothed it, and then returned to her mirror to brush her hair vigorously. It was light brown in colour, and curled naturally when she let it. Now, she coaxed it into ringlets and caught them up on her crown with the ribbon, leaving a few little curls about her face. Even to her own critical eyes she looked quite pretty.

A pair of blue velvet slippers and her only pair of white kid gloves completed the ensemble, and then she stood by the bed, breathing slowly to steady herself, and looking at the shawl. It was very beautiful. Of course, she must return it to him. A chilling vision of the long, lonely days ahead entered her mind, and she thought how comforting it would be to have something to remind her that someone had once been kind enough to give her a pretty gift, and somehow, without really coming to a conscious decision about it, she picked it up and placed it round her shoulders. Then, having checked that she had a clean handkerchief, she snuffed out the candles and left the room.

The landing was lit by another branch of candles on a wide shelf near the staircase. Their light reflected softly on the golden glory of Sir Richard's mess-dress as he leaned against the wall opposite her door, his face in the shadows. Her immediate reaction was to turn round and go back into her room, but he said softly, "Don't run away, Dorcas!"

She stopped, half-turned away from him, holding tightly on to the door-knob.

"Please allow me to apologise, at least."

She was silent, unable to look at him, or move.

"I didn't mean to do it," he said, sounding anxious and a little bewildered. "I'm not in the habit of leaping on unprotected females like that, and it certainly wasn't because I was thinking along the same lines as our Mr. Black! I mean, I don't think you're the sort of young lady who welcomes, or even allows a fellow to take liberties."

She made a slight movement, which apparently gave him the impression that she was questioning this assertion, for he went on quite indignantly, "I'm not such a fool as to mistake you for anything other than what you are—a gentlewoman of quality and breeding—and I'm very sorry if I've led you to think otherwise! I respect you, and—and what happened was in no way insulting to you! I'm sorry I frightened you, and I beg your pardon most abjectly! I'd go on my knees if I could."

She gave him a wary, sidelong look. He certainly appeared very contrite.

"You stole my hairpins!" she said unsteadily.

At once, he held them out to her in one immaculately white-gloved hand. They were neatly bunched together and tied with a scrap of red ribbon. She took them and dropped them into her reticule, murmuring, "Thank you."

"I had a very strong wish to see your hair loose," he said earnestly. "It curls, just as I suspected! Why do you restrain it so severely, when it looks so pretty loose?"

"A governess is not expected to wear her hair in curls," she replied, that slight bitterness creeping into her voice.

"May I hope you might accept my apology?" he asked diffidently.

'Yes," very quietly.

"Thank you."

There was an awkward silence. Miss Minster kept her eyes firmly on the clasp of her reticule, which she clutched in both hands, and Sir Richard was trying unobtrusively to see her face in the dim light.

"Are we to stand here all evening?" he asked eventually.

Miss Minster became aware that there were sounds of bustling activity downstairs. Two or three people were scurrying back and forth in the hall, and voices were uplifted in song in the tap-room. The door next to hers opened suddenly, and Mr. Petts emerged, resplendent in blue broadcloth, a canary waistcoat and nankeen pantaloons.

"You stand there as long as you like, me buck!" he said affably, "but, if you'll excuse me, I'm for roast goose!" and he ran lightly down the stairs.

Whatever spell had held Miss Minster immovable was broken by this interruption. She closed her door and walked quite naturally past Sir Richard to the stairs, and began to descend. Halfway down, she checked and looked back. Sir Richard had just reached the top step.

"Thank you for the shawl. It's very beautiful," she said in a low, gentle voice.

"I'm glad you like it." He was wondering how much Mr. Petts had overheard.

Miss Minster had the same anxiety, but when she entered the dining-room, Mr. Petts was standing by the fireplace contemplating his own boots and saying nothing, and gave not the slightest sign thereafter that he had heard anything at all of the conversation on the landing. The maids were busy loading the table with covered dishes wherever they could find room between the cutlery, glasses and bottles already set out. Mr. Tupper was watching with great interest, and seemed to be suffering from a little too much starch in the high collar and cravat he had donned in honour of the occasion. He looked at Miss Minster over his spectacles and said shyly, "How pretty you look, my dear young lady!"

She dropped him a smiling curtsey and moved towards the window, unconsciously turning to look back towards the door, and was quite surprised when Mr. Black came in next, rubbing his hands briskly and exclaiming, "Ain't they ready yet? I 'ope it's worth the wait!"

He caught sight of Miss Minster and surveyed her with his usual leer, saying, "You took my adwice, then! Very pretty, if I'm allowed to say so!"

"Well you ain't, so don't!" Sir Richard said austerely almost in his ear, having entered behind him. Mr. Black started and scowled, but went to inspect the table without saying anything.

"I hope I may be allowed to speak on the subject!" Mr. Kirby said from the parlour doorway. "You are exquisite, dear lady! Quite exquisite!" and he advanced the length of the room, smilingly handsome, his blue eyes frankly admiring her, to kiss her hand, at which a becoming touch of colour appeared in her cheeks and she smiled. Sir Richard suddenly mouthed an abrupt swearword, having apparently hurt his knee by standing awkwardly, and limped to the head of the table.

The landlady appeared next, very flushed and perspiring, bobbed a curtsey to the assembled Quality—if Mr. Black could be classified as such—and said something breathlessly in her incomprehensible dialect about things being "scrowy" and "hapsherapsher", and finished with what they took to be an invitation to be seated at the table. Then she whisked out and was replaced by Jem and the maids.

Sir Richard took the head of the table as usual, with an unaffected naturalness which showed no particular consciousness of his social superiority over his companions, and invited Miss Minster to her place on his right with a smiling gesture, Jem shooting forward to hold her chair in a very officious manner, beating Mr. Kirby to it by a short head. That defeated gentleman made certain of his seat on Miss Minster's right by sidestepping in front of Mr. Black, who appeared about to usurp it, and diverted the thief-taker to the foot of the table, with Mr. Petts on the other side of him, so that Mr. Tupper found himself promoted to Sir Richard's left.

After Sir Richard had said a short grace, the meal began with mutton broth, and then the covers were removed to reveal a magnificent goose, a joint of beef, a raised pie, a ham, both roast and boiled potatoes, cabbage, and buttered parsnips. Sir Richard carved the goose with great aplomb, causing Mr. Tupper to exclaim, "Ah, what it is to have skill in carving! I fear I make but a sorry job of it with poultry, 'though I can manage a saddle of mutton or a round of beef well enough! I suppose it must be a matter of practice, sir?"

"Never carved a goose before in m'life!" Sir Richard replied cheerfully. "If I'm succeeding, it's a combination of common sense and good luck!"

He arranged several choice slices of breast on a plate and presented it to Miss Minster, who could not help contrasting his idea of a lady's helping to the meagre, half-cold leavings which had constituted her lonely Christmas dinner last year.

"Wing or leg?" Sir Richard asked Mr. Tupper, who was suddenly overcome by the realisation that he was being served by a real baronet, and replied, "A *small* wing, if you please!" which put Sir Richard in a quandary, as both wings were of the same large size. He considered the matter for a moment, then said firmly, "This is the smallest," and placed the first which came to hand on Mr. Tupper's plate.

"I'll have a leg!" Mr. Black declared, without waiting to be asked.

"What for you, Mr. Kirby?" Sir Richard asked, ignoring him.

"A little white meat, and some of this beef, if you please," Mr. Kirby replied politely, slicing the beef himself as it was immediately before him.

Mr. Petts was invited to specify his wishes next, and replied, "I would like some dark meat, if you would be so kind," a speech of unusual length for him, perhaps in order to disassociate himself from his uncouth neighbour. Sir Richard found him a generous helping, and then cut off a leg and served it to Mr. Black without a word. Jem passed the plates and the maids handed the vegetables.

"Covess was worriting abaht 'aving no fish," Jem informed them. "I tole 'er you'd not mind."

"Quite right," Sir Richard assured him. "It's an excellent meal, and we're much obliged to her."

He carved himself a few slices of breast, and put a small pile of assorted fragments on the side of his plate. Miss Minster noticed that he was quite a light eater, for he took only a small amount of vegetables instead of piling his plate as the others did, and then ate slowly, so that he did not finish before them. From time to time, he picked up one of the oddments in his right hand, which then disappeared under the table with it. Miss Minster glanced down, and was not surprised to see the cat Maurice seated close beside him, looking up expectantly.

"I could 'ave fancied a neel pie," Mr. Black observed, but no-one bothered to reply, except that both Mr. Petts and Mr. Kirby gave him a cold look.

There was a selection of bottles on the table, some of them with handwritten labels, which proved to be parsnip and elderflower wines of the landlord's own making. Sir Richard tasted the latter, pronounced it very palatable, and invited Miss Minster to take a glass of it. She accepted, and knowing that it could be very potent, sipped it cautiously, and found it pleasant and not too strong. Mr. Tupper expressed a preference for port, which was also Mr. Kirby's choice, and the other two took ale.

"It ain't bad, is it?" Sir Richard asked Miss Minster anxiously.

"It's really very good," she replied. "And it will please the landlord if we drink some of it." She saw from the quick glance he gave her that this was precisely his reason for taking it.

There was a marked lack of conversation for some time as they worked steadily through the food before them, and then Sir Richard enquired if anyone would care for a little more goose. Miss Minster smilingly declined. Mr. Tupper allowed himself to be persuaded to a trifle of breast, Mr. Petts expressed a preference for beef, Mr. Kirby tried the ham, and Mr. Black decided to broach the pie. He cut himself a large slice, and found it was veal and ham, with a light, lardy crust and hardboiled eggs among the meat.

"I likes to see a pie cut into," he volunteered through a mouthful of it. "Sets me in mind of Newman's 'Otel, all whitewashed over, wi' a great 'ole in its walls!"

"That's an odd sentiment," Miss Minster observed. "Fancy a thief-taker wishing to see Newgate Gaol with its walls breached!"

Mr. Black laughed and choked on his pie. Mr. Petts helpfully banged him on the back until he recovered and took a swallow of ale.

"The more thiefs is loose, the more there is to take!" he explained.

"Ah! You're in it for the money!" Mr. Petts said gloomily.

"What else, cully? Forty pahnd for a 'Ightobyman— Ten pahnd for you, if I catches you borrowing a pad!"

"What about the suppression of evil and the protection of the honest citizen?" Sir Richard enquired. "After all, a man who steals, for instance, is taking what is not his from someone who may have worked very hard to obtain whatever is stolen from him. Surely an honest person has a right to be protected in the enjoyment of his own property?"

Mr. Black sniffed. "Them as 'as property 'as usually got it by taking it from somebody else. 'Ow did you come by your bit o' land?" pointing his fork at Sir Richard.

"By inheritance, mainly," Sir Richard replied good-humouredly, but there was a slight tightening in the muscles about his mouth.

"So what 'ave you done to *earn* it, then? Spent your time gallyvanting about the Continent in your pretty uniform, 'aving a good time with the senoritas, whiles your servants does all the work what gives you the bunts to buy your pair o' colours! Oh yes, *somebody* works, but it ain't you and your kind!"

"Damned impertinence!" exclaimed Mr. Kirby irately, but Miss Minster cut in and said in the clear, cold voice with which she was wont to correct an ill-mannered child, "If it were not for the gallant officers of the Army and Navy, we should by now be in the same condition of abject slavery that the rest of Europe has suffered all these years! You forget, Mr. Black, that Sir Richard was wounded in the service of his country—our country— *your* country, sir! You choose to mock at his lameness and speak slightingly of the position in life to which he was born, but may I ask what you have ever done to defend your country? What action have you taken against Bonaparte? What have you done for mankind, other than sell your less fortunate compatriots to the gallows?"

She recollected herself at this point and broke off, blushing most becomingly. There was a stunned silence for a moment, and Mr. Black stared at her with his mouth half-open, looking like a stranded cod. Then Mr. Petts clapped his hands together two or three times and said "Bravo!" Jem nodded and volunteered "Well said, Miss!" and Mr. Kirby gazed admiringly at her and murmured "Well! I Say!" Mr. Tupper blew his nose loudly and bravely agreed, "Very well said, my dear young lady!" and Sir Richard looked vastly amused and murmured "Best since Mr. Pitt!" then added more loudly, "May I, on behalf of my brother-officers of both Services, thank you for your spirited defence, Madam?" He stood up, raised his glass, and drained it to her, then sat down again. Miss Minster blushed still more.

Mr. Black looked distinctly uncomfortable and shut his mouth, then opened it again to say grudgingly, "Well, no offence intended to anyone 'ere present. I daresay I got carried away, and I begs your pardon, but to tell truth, landowners sticks in me gullet, with their Game Laws and their 'igh and mighty ways! 'Alf the thiefs what ends up on the gallows only comes to it through poaching or through losing their liveli'ood through enclosures, and that's all down to *landlords*!''

"Quite true," Sir Richard said mildly. "I agree with what you say, and I accept your apology. Now, may we drop the subject? It's hardly suitable for Christmas! A glass of wine with you, Mr. Black!" He raised his refilled glass in a toast, and Mr. Black responded with good grace. Other toasts followed, and Miss Minster was the recipient of several of them, which she acknowledged with a graceful inclination of the head, a little surprised by the admiring looks which accompanied some of them. She was unaware that the warmth of the room, the landlord's wine and her spirited attack on Mr. Black had combined to give her an unaccustomed sparkle and colour which showed what a Beauty she might have been had the circumstances of her life been more fortunate. Sir Richard leaned back in his chair, having finished his beef, and watched the effect she was having on the other men with a glint of amusement, which turned to a slight irritation as he observed the ardency with which Mr. Kirby, having possessed himself of the lady's right hand, pressed it to his lips and murmured some pleasantry which caused her to withdraw the hand and shake her head reprovingly. Mr. Kirby did not, however, appear to be much put down by this, and continued to give her his exclusive attention, except for a brief interval when the cat Maurice took a short stroll and attempted to strop his claws on the young gentleman's riding-boot. This attention was not appreciated, and the indignant animal returned to his more reliable friend, who absentmindedly rewarded him with a whole slice of beef.

CHAPTER SEVEN

WHEN THE DINERS felt that they had demolished sufficient of the main course, Sir Richard gave Jem the nod and the servants cleared the dishes. Then they brought in clean plates, a large jug of custard—smelling strongly of brandy—two jellies moulded like castles, and a pink blancmanger. There was a short hiatus, and then steps were heard in the hall, Jem opened the door with one of his flourishes, and the landlord entered, red-faced and beaming, with the Pudding!

It was worthy of the capital letter. It was round and dark, rich with plums and suet, steaming fragrantly, crowned with a sprig of holly bright with berries, and the diners gave it a spontaneous round of applause. The landlord conveyed it safely to the table, and placed it before Sir Richard, who inspected it admiringly, and exclaimed, "What an excellent pudding! You're a lucky man, landlord, to be married to such a cook!"

"Oh, aye!" the landlord agreed, patting his round belly. "Ah'll allow she'm a gradely cook!" He took a glass of wine with them, at Sir Richard's invitation, to toast the pudding, and then withdrew, bowing a great many times, and backing out of the presence of the Quality.

Sir Richard removed the holly and presented it to Miss Minster with a courtly bow, and then squared up to the pudding with knife and spoon. It cut beautifully, being neither soggy nor too dry.

"A small piece please!" Miss Minster said hurriedly when she saw where Sir Richard's second cut was taking him, for she was already near repletion with goose and vegetables. He obligingly halved the quantity he had first estimated, but she still thought it very large, and looked at it with misgiving. Jem appeared at her elbow and concealed it under a ladleful of brandy sauce, which he served with enthusiasm and liberality, while Sir Richard went on to serve man-sized slices to the others.

It was as delicious as it looked. They all said it was the best pudding they had ever tasted, but no-one was capable of a second helping, or even of toying with the jelly or blancmanger, for its richness was particularly filling.

"I trust there's another for you, Jem?" Sir Richard said, surveying the wreckage.

"Bless you, yes! Us'll get urn arterwards. There's another goose, bigger'n yourn, and two-three puddings bin a-boiling in the copper all day. We gets done prahd in the kitchen! Beat's cockfighting!"

After the debris of the pudding had been removed, there was still dessert to follow. A large bowl of apples— a trifle wizened, but still sweet and sound—a bowl of walnuts, mincepies, sugar comfits, almond biscuits, sugar-plums, a large crumbly cheese and crusty bread and butter for anyone who still felt hungry. Some more port, a stone bottle of cherry brandy and a couple of bottles of cognac with unashamedly French labels were brought too, and everyone pushed back from the table a little, with some surreptitious loosening of waistbands in one or two cases. Mr. Kirby, who had already consumed a fair quantity of port, tugged absentmindedly at his neckcloth and thereby ruined a creation which had cost him half an hour of concentrated effort.

Miss Minster made to rise, intending to leave the gentlemen to their port, but Sir Richard said, "Oh, don't go away! You'll be all alone in the parlour. Stay and take a little cherry brandy—it looks the genuine article."

"Smuggled?" Miss Minster enquired, resuming her place.

"Well, we ain't been importing any legally for some time!" Sir Richard replied, pouring her a generous half-tumbler. "Walnuts?"

"There don't appear to be any nutcrackers," she replied, looking round for them, but both her neighbours reached for a couple and showed her that they could be cracked one against the other, Sir Richard with more success than Mr. Kirby, who rather fumbled the job. Mr. Tupper peeled himself an apple, and contrived with much concentration to take all the skin off in one long strip.

"In my young days," he said, "we used to do this and try to divine whom we should marry. Only in fun, of course."

"How do you do that?" asked Sir Richard, taking an apple.

"You must take off the skin, as I have done, without breaking the strip, then take it by one end and twirl it three times round your head, and let it fall, so. It should form the initial letter of your future partner's name." He demonstrated as he spoke, but the peel landed in a neat spiral. "It doesn't work for me, of course, for I have already been married," he explained.

Sir Richard carefully peeled his apple, and tried his luck. His strip of peel broke in two as it landed, and he tried to make something of the result. "It looks like an I and a back-to-front C."

"They're almost touching, so it could be a D," Mr. Petts said in his most expressionless manner, caught Sir Richard's eye and winked solemnly, receiving an inscrutable look in reply. Miss Minster was peeling her own apple and did not observe it.

Her attempt failed, as she could not manage to take off the peel in one piece, for the elderflower wine and the brandy were not compatible, and her hands were not as steady as they might have been. Mr. Kirby was in a worse case, for he cut his finger and dropped his apple on the floor, where it was promptly commandeered and batted smartly about the room by the cat Maurice in playful mood. Mr. Kirby uttered a sharp "Damn!" and thrust his finger into his mouth, then removed it to apologise to Miss Minster. Fortunately, one of the maids brought in the teatray soon after, and served them all a sobering cup of strong brew.

"Jem tells me there is to be some kind of entertainment in the tap-room later on," Sir Richard remarked. "It might be amusing to look in on it, I think?"

The others agreed, and later on, when a tramping of feet in the hall indicated that the servants had finished their dinner in the kitchen, the parlour party joined them in the tap-room, which had been rearranged for the occasion, with the tables and benches pushed back nearer the walls to leave a clear space in the middle. A few chairs had been set at the window end for the Quality, and Mr. Kirby handed Miss Minster to one of them, seating himself on her right, while Sir Richard and the cat Maurice took her other side, the latter on the former's good knee, and Mr. Tupper sat next to them. Mr. Black went to the other end, by the bar, and sat at a table with a wiry, brown-faced lad with curly black hair, whom Miss Minster had seen about the yard and assumed to be the stable-lad. He seemed to be on very good terms with Mr. Black, to judge from the way they were talking and laughing. Mr. Petts settled himself at the end of the next bench to them, folded his arms, and leaned back against the wall.

There were a couple of dozen people in the big room, some of them employed at the inn, and others from somewhere fairly near at hand—presumably outlying cottages and farms, for there was no village hereabouts. One of them was the coach-driver, seeming very cheerful, with his bandaged ankle resting on a hassock, with a couple of chairs arranged to save him from any accidental knocks, and a steady supply of pots of ale at his elbow. Another was the old shepherd who had read the lesson in church, still with his dog at his side, watching the proceedings with great interest. It exchanged a few mild insults with the cat Maurice, but after that, the two animals studiously ignored each other's existence.

The room had been decorated, like the rest of the public rooms, with garlands of holly, ivy and ribbons along the dark beams, and a huge log, practically an entire tree-trunk, burning in the hearth. The company was in a jolly frame of mind, red-faced and beaming with seasonal good-will, goose and the landlord's best brew.

The shepherd had brought his fiddle, and after a few preliminary scratchings and tunings, struck up a lively jig. The landlady, the maids, and a couple of young girls who probably helped in the kitchen, were soon persuaded by the men to get up and dance, and a dozen couples pranced and stamped on the stone flats, thoroughly enjoying themselves for all that they showed more energy than grace.

Sir Richard tapped his foot in time to the music and called for ale all round when the dance ended, thereby ensuring that the visiting "off-comes" were regarded in a more friendly fashion than they had been at first, when a few doubtful looks had been cast in their direction. There was a great deal of "Good 'ealth too 'ee, sir!" as the ale slid down thirsty throats, and some pleasant smiles thereafter. Miss Minster suspected that they had thought the visitors had come to make fun of their simple pleasures, and so she was not displeased when the shepherd next struck up "Sir Roger", and Mr. Kirby sprang to his feet, seized her hand and begged her to stand up with him for the dance.

She was light on her feet and enjoyed dancing, swinging down the middle, laughing and with curls bobbing, when it came to their turn, and moving with a charming natural grace in contrast to the bouncing and stamping of the others, particularly Jem, who was doing his ungainly best and being pulled and pushed by his giggling partner whenever he went astray, which was at least twice in every figure. Sir Richard noted with a certain sardonic satisfaction that Mr. Kirby was not much gifted as a dancer, and gave the impression that his boots were too tight, or possibly joined together by a short length of invisible string. When the dance ended and Miss Minster returned to her seat, flushed and animated, he greeted her with a reflection of her own smile, half-rising in courtesy, with a firm hand on his feline companion to prevent it falling off his knee.

"You enjoy dancing," he stated rather than asked.

She hesitated a little too long, seeking a tactful reply, for it seemed, under the circumstances, unkind to say simply, "Yes."

"I seldom have the opportunity," she eventually replied evasively.

"But you enjoy it?"

"Well, yes, but as I enjoy other things—walking, or riding, or reading. I should not wish to spend all my time at it."

"No, I suppose not," he said reflectively. "Somehow, one takes one's enjoyments rather for granted until one no longer has the ability..."

"Did you enjoy dancing, then?" she asked cautiously.

"Yes, but not passionately. I suppose I didn't think much about it when I could, and it's only now that I can't that it becomes at all important." He gave her a rueful, self-deprecating smile. "Stupid, ain't it?"

"No. Just human and natural."

"Human and natural things ain't always acceptable to other people, self-pity, or whatever else... Because one has a strong but entirely natural urge to do something, any other person involved may not consider it so, and be dam-deuced annoyed about it!" He said this apparently to the cat's right ear, but it was plain to Miss Minster that he was not referring to dancing, but to a particular and fairly recent event, and she did not know how to answer him, for she had firmly not allowed herself to think about it until she should be alone and have time to attend to it properly.

"I haven't really had a chance to consider the matter," she replied in a low, hurried voice. "But I think it is probably best forgotten..." She sounded agitated and worried.

"Yes," he replied briefly.

"Something worrying you, my dear lady?" Mr. Kirby enquired in honeyed tones in her other ear. "You look disturbed."

"No, not at all," she replied. "I was just catching my breath."

There was now some hearty singing going on, and after that, more dancing. Mr. Kirby stood up with Miss Minster for some of the simpler country dances, but owned himself not much acquainted with the figures of most of them. When everyone felt in need for a breather, two strapping fellows were persuaded to pull off their coats and take the centre of the floor for a bout of wrestling.

Miss Minster had never seen wrestling before, but the gentlemen expressed great interest, for it was a variety new to the Southerners. Mr. Tupper explained that it was peculiar to Cumberland and Westmoreland, and required skill and agility rather than strength. He kept up a commentary throughout the match which showed him to be something of a connoisseur.

The two men faced one another, and each placed one arm over his opponent's shoulder, and the other arm around his waist, and linked his hands behind the other's back, and, at a word from the landlord, who was acting as judge, they began to twist, not breaking their handclasps, but stamping hard on the floor, each feeling for a chance to trip, or throw the other off balance. The audience watched with close interest, offering advice and encouragement, applauding a good move with cries of "Bai!" and the banging of pintpots on tables. After more than ten minutes of what Mr. Tupper described variously as "swinging hipe" and "grand-step", one of the wrestlers gave a sudden heave, caught the other over his hip in some extraordinary fashion, and dropped him with a crash on the floor. "Cross-buttock!" announced Mr. Tupper.

That was the end of the match, the object having been simply for one man to make the other touch the ground with some part of himself other than his feet. Victor and vanquished were refreshed with ale, and a certain amount of coin changed hands around the room.

"I reckons I could do that!" exclaimed Jem.

"Coom on, then!" the winner offered, grinning, and Jem stripped off his coat, flexed his arms, and advanced to battle. The landlord explained the rules to him and meanwhile a number of wagers were laid, not all for one side.

"Give him a trial run first!" Sir Richard suggested, and this was accepted as very fair. The two wrestlers took up their positions and began to feel for advantage, feet shifting and seeking ankles, pelvises twisting as they changed weight and tried each other's balance.

After a few minutes, Jem said he had the idea, and the struggle began in earnest. The local man—"'Arry to his friends"—tried contemptuously to sweep Jem's feet from under him, and was obviously surprised to find the Londoner standing firm and almost catching him off balance himself.

"Jem must always try every new experience!" Sir Richard said quietly to Miss Minster. "He even essayed bull-fighting in Spain! He didn't win, but he gave the bull a few surprises, and managed to escape without being gored, which was quite an achievement!"

Jem grinned at his opponent's discomfiture, and said, "It ain't too 'ard, is it?" and then suddenly flew over the other's back and landed with a thud on the floor. 'Arry gave him a hand up and let him have another go, and this time, Jem came very near to winning, but the bout ended with the novice recumbent once more and laughing uproariously at his own downfall. His opponent pulled him up again, and bought him a consolatory pot of ale, having obviously taken a liking to him, and they spent some time deep in conversation about the gentle art, which, as Jem admitted "''as more to it than yer'd fink!"

After some more dancing and singing, trays of mince pies and slices of cold pudding were handed round, and the small horse-collar from the hall brought in for a gurning competition. The idea of this appeared to be for each contestant to don the collar and pull the most hideous face he could manage. Mr. Tupper and Sir Richard sportingly took a turn, but Mr. Kirby declined with some annoyance at first, then allowed himself to be persuaded by Miss Minster. Mr. Black ungraciously pushed the collar away when it was offered to him, with a sneering comment, but Mr. Petts accepted it, and to everyone's surprise, produced a grimace of such magnificent hideousness that he was adjudged the winner. Jem, of course, was eager to take a turn but laughed too much to do more than squint and look like a cross-eyed hedgehog.

The party eventually broke up after midnight, by which time many of the merrymakers were asleep with hands on the tables. Those who lived at the inn bustled about clearing up under the remarkably sober eye of the landlord, and the others went off home, singing and laughing as they meandered unsteadily away.

Miss Minster, feeling almost stifled by the hot and stuffy atmosphere of the tap-room, stepped out into the porch before the front door for a breath of air, and stood watching the lanterns bobbing away over the snow, and listening to the merry strains of the fiddle as the old shepherd trudged up the hillside, still playing away, his dog dancing around him in the moonlight.

"As merry a Christmas as I've spent in a long time, I do believe!" Sir Richard remarked quietly behind her, making her start as she had not heard him follow her.

"Yes, a very pleasant day," she replied, and then, recalling one incident in the course of it, hoped he had not misunderstood her.

"And a wonderful night! Look at the sky!"

She looked up. Above the bulk of Helvellyn, the sky was black velvet set with diamonds, and a near-full moon lit everything in crisp white and black. They stood for a few moments looking, and then he put a comradely arm about her shoulders, and said, "Don't take cold, m'dear!"

She jerked away from him as if she had been stung, dislodging the arm, and turned to go indoors, but he was standing squarely in her way. The light behind him in the hall set his outline in silhouette, and she noticed inconsequentially that he looked oddly deformed about the neck. Then she realised that he was, so to speak, wearing the cat Maurice.

"You needn't run off like a startled hare! I'm not about to seize you and carry you off to my mountain fastness, in order to hold you subject to my wicked will, you know!" He sounded mildly amused. "There's something I wish to say to you, if I may, before you sweep past me in disdain."

"What is it?" she asked, feeling very foolish.

"Thank you for speaking up in my defence at dinner."

"Oh, it was nothing. He annoyed me, for what he said was unfair and—and unnecessary. Besides, I was afraid you would take offence and . . ." she broke off.

"And what? Call him out?"

"Yes."

"I couldn't do that. He ain't a gentleman!"

"Oh. No, I suppose not."

"In any case, I'm a peaceable sort of fellow—I don't go about calling people out. You can't really blame him for his feelings, for what he said was true enough, and as for denigrating what the Army is up to abroad—well, he's obviously not over-gifted with imagination, and he has no idea what field-service is really like, or how an army looks after a hard battle. He's never seen a village after the French have left it, with everything and everyone broken—unarmed men hacked to death, and women, even little girls . . .'' He broke off without saying ''raped'', but Miss Minster guessed what he meant from the anguished tone of his voice. ''All he sees is taxes going up every year, and soldiers on leave peacocking about and stealing all the women! And the enclosures—he's right there too! They have to come, to make one acre grow what took three before, but the poor suffer by them, there's no denying, and the loss of common rights and a bit of land to grow enough for his family does drive many a poor country fellow to crime. There'll be the devil to pay when the war is over, unless someone finds a way to mend matters! Still, for all that he's right, Black was quite excessively offensive, and if he's a Runner, I'm on the side of our highwayman!''

''I wonder where he is?'' Miss Minster mused.

''Who? Black Beelzebub? Well, now—I'd say either just gone up to the room next to yours, or possibly out in the stable with Jem, in committee over a lame mare!''

''Mr. Kirby?'' She sounded shocked.

''Why not? He's tall and slim-built, well-set up shoulders, and speaks like a Southerner, and we've only his word that he owns an estate by Keswick.''

''But he's a gentleman!''

Sir Richard laughed. ''He wouldn't be the first gentleman who's taken to the High Toby, either for amusement, or to cover the gap between his income and his expenditure!''

"You're joking!"

"No, not entirely. Don't let his blue eyes and handsome face blind you to the possibility that he might be a villain!"

Miss Minster considered this, and was inclined to dismiss the idea of Mr. Kirby as a highwayman as absurd, except that some tiny, buried section of her mind faintly signalled disquiet, but for what reason she could not imagine.

"Which reminds me," Sir Richard went on mildly, "that I wished to say to you that you've really no need to be afraid of me, you know! I ain't a villain—or not entirely, despite my lame leg, for I've not had it long enough to develop the correct degree of wickedness to go with it! I ain't inclined to force any female to do anything she don't wish to do—'though I might try a little gentle persuasion, I'll admit!" he added reflectively. "I really think you should go in now, before you become chilled. Don't forget you ain't got half a ton of hot cat to keep the cold out!"

Miss Minster, who was beginning to feel cold, obediently slipped past him and went in, calling "Goodnight!" to the busy figures in the tap-room as she passed. She climbed the stairs, with Sir Richard, having rid himself of his sleepy muffler by depositing it on the hall table, where it yawned pinkly and curled up in a tidy ball, following her up. At the top of the flight, he said, "Pleasant dreams, Dorcas!"

She paused with her hand on the knob of her own door, and replied, "Goodnight, Richard." She had meant to say "*Sir* Richard" but the title somehow got lost on the way, and the resultant confusion made her whisk into the room and shut the door with unnecessary force, turning the key in the lock without really noticing she had done so.

The fire had been made up recently, and the bed turned down, with a hot brick slipped between the sheets. She undressed and washed, then snuffed out the candles and snuggled down in the feather mattress, cuddling the brick, and soon felt warm and comfortable in her body, but certainly not in her mind, which was at last free to consider Sir Richard's extraordinary behaviour.

Not that she really wanted to think about it. She felt so confused, half-excited, half-frightened, puzzled, and thoroughly thrown out of balance by the recollection of the violent effect of his kiss on her own mind and body, that she would rather have dismissed the whole incident as a disturbing dream, or a nightmare. However, it had been waiting in the back of her mind all the evening, threatening to take on the dimensions of a major disaster, and common-sense told her that it must be reduced to its proper proportions.

The trouble was, that she was unable to dismiss it as merely a kiss, a piece of opportunism on the part of an amorously inclined young man, and nothing of any importance, because it was not the first time she had been kissed, and yet it differed to such an enormous extent from her earlier experiences that she could not understand what had happened. Certainly, it was not in the same universe as that wet, sticky affair in the stableyard when she was fourteen, or even the more competent attempt by a young dandy at her first and only ball. As for the furtive fumblings of a lecherous elderly visitor to the house where she was a governess, or the brash, clumsy and unsuccessful efforts by the son of the same house—nothing in her experience had been anything like the shock she had received today.

She found herself trembling at the remembrance of it, recalling the strange, hollow feeling, half excitement, half fear, part longing, the curious yearning ache in her body when it ended. Did Sir Richard know he could arouse such feelings in her? Was it usual for a woman to feel so, if she was kissed like that? He must have guessed something, at least—that was evident from his apology. Perhaps he had assumed that she would know what to expect, but, if so, then he must have thought her to be the sort of female who allowed men to kiss her...

She suddenly found herself crying, tears running freely down her cheeks, at the idea that he might have thought her a loose woman, or that he might be the sort of man who went about kissing, or worse, any woman who caught his fancy! This was somehow mixed up with the fear that he might think her a prude, and that he might be a dissolute rake who only pretended to be kind and pleasant to disarm his intended victims. It was very depressing, confusing and entirely illogical, and required several stern admonishments to herself about silliness and some rather confused prayers which were internally self-contradictory, before she could calm herself sufficiently for her genuine fatigue to intervene and allow her to fall asleep.

She dreamed alarmingly, that she was being abducted by Sir Richard, mounted on a horse-sized ginger cat which arched its eyebrows and looked down its beaky nose at her as it galloped along a narrow icy ledge in the midst of a harshly serrated mountain range, with Jem's disembodied voice exhorting her or Sir Richard to keep going because the sea was not far off, and the ice was fit for skating, and the Game Laws would not permit Mr. Kirby to shoot them, and there was Mr. Kirby, dressed as a highwayman, pursuing them on a huge black horse, flying wildly through the frighteningly jagged and ugly scenery and shouting something about wishing to dance with her!

It was a considerable relief to wake up and find it was only a dream!

After that, she composed herself by reciting the Twenty-third Psalm, which seemed appropriate, the first two or three pages of *Paradise Lost*, declined the Latin noun *mensa*—a table, and fell asleep again halfway through dealing in a similar way with *canis*—a dog, and this time dreamt only fleetingly of the sheep-dog dancing in the snow.

In the morning, she was a little nervous at the thought of encountering Sir Richard again, and unconsciously prepared herself by arranging her hair in her most governessy and plain fashion, then rebelled and rearranged it in a chignon and curls instead, as if she were still the daughter of a baronet and not obliged to support herself by earning a salary. When she eventually went down, she found him at breakfast, looking no more satanic or cloven-footed than before, and just as pleasantly affable as ever. He smiled approvingly at her hair, but only remarked that it was a fine, bright morning, and much less cold, and that the snow was now melting in a satisfactory fashion, as, indeed, a steady dripping from the eves of the inn indicated. She replied in kind, as if nothing untoward had occurred between them at all.

"You going shooting?" Mr. Petts enquired.

"Yes, rather!" Mr. Kirby replied with enthusiasm, even turning away from Miss Minster for a moment, while Sir Richard said, "I suppose so," with much less enthusiasm, going on, "I don't much care for the mass slaughter of harmless creatures, but I can hardly disoblige our landlady. Care to come?"

"No, thankee," Mr. Petts replied briefly.

Sir Richard looked enquiringly at Mr. Tupper, who exclaimed, "I can't abide firearms! Nasty, dangerous things!'' Mr. Black appeared to be deeply engrossed in a large bowl of porridge, and Sir Richard did not extend the invitation to him, but turned to Miss Minster a fraction after Mr. Kirby said to her, with a beguiling smile and a coaxing tone, ''You'll come, won't you?''

''I'd like a little fresh air and exercise, but I've no wish to be in the way.''

''You won't be, as long as you stay where I tell you and don't screech when the guns go off,'' Sir Richard cut in neatly, ''and I'm sure you're too commonsensical for that!''

And so, soon after breakfast, Miss Minster found herself, well-wrapped up, sitting between Mr. Kirby and Sir Richard on the sledge, while Jem plodded along leading the horse, and the two gentlemen argued the merits of their respective gunsmiths over her head. Mr. Kirby favoured Wogan, and had a spanking new pair in a fine walnut case which looked as if it had never been so much as opened before, while Sir Richard swore by Manton, and had a pair of his shotguns, beautifully engraved about the breech with ''Joseph Manton'' and a fine flourish of curlicues. Their stocks showed the polish of much use, and their case was a handsome rosewood one, inlaid with silver, but much battered and bruised, with a long gouge across the top, as if a bullet had ploughed a furrow across it.

While the discussion progressed, Sir Richard checked the contents of the case methodically, and then set about mounting the barrels on the stocks and measuring powder and shot for the charges.

''Yer won't find nuffing missing!'' Jem remarked pointedly at the beginning of the operation. ''I checked 'em meself afore we come aht.''

"Only a fool leaves the checking of guns to another," Sir Richard replied.

They went across the head of the lake on a cart-track, ruts already showing through the snow, and bumped across little stone bridges over the two streams which ran down from the slopes above the Dunmail road. The snow had melted in patches, leaving a few areas of grass clear. Icicles still hung on the sallows and rushes by the streams. A large number of assorted wildfowl could be seen feeding on the marshy area where the streams spread out before disappearing into the still-frozen lake.

CHAPTER EIGHT

JEM SELECTED A SPOT well within range of the wildfowl and concealed from them by a clump of bushes, cast off the sledge there, and took the horse well out of the arc of fire and tethered it on a fairly large area of grass which was free from snow. Miss Minster removed herself from the back of the sledge out of the way, and watched the gentlemen load their guns. She noticed that Sir Richard seemed to go about it with much more concentration than Mr. Kirby, and completed the task in considerably the shorter time, and thought that it must be the result of having done it at times when his life depended on speed and care in reloading.

She noticed that the slopes rising behind them were only thinly adorned with snow, and in many places were quite free of it, being, she supposed, in the lee of the high ridge, and also exposed to the morning sun, and before the shooting began, she said, "Would it be convenient for me to walk about on the hillside, if I keep at some distance behind you?"

Mr. Kirby immediately asked in disappointed tones if she would not prefer to sit and watch the shooting, but Sir Richard looked to see where she was thinking of going, and replied, "Yes, by all means, but try to avoid making a noise, and see that you keep out of our line of fire—I mean, stay on the hillside and don't go wandering down to the lake. I'd not care to have you served up, stuffed and roasted, for dinner tomorrow!"

Miss Minster smiled at the idea, and picked her way up the slope to the foot of the steeper rise, and wandered about for a time among the clumps of trees and scattered rocks, avoiding the patches of snow, and looking about at the lichens and pine-cones, the draggled remains of last year's flowers, and the occasional first green shoots of the coming summer. At intervals, she heard the double bang as one of the gentlemen fired both barrels, and the flurry of wings followed until the birds settled again. Half-unconsciously, she noted that there was a difference in sound between the two pairs of guns, and that one seemed to fire more frequently than the other.

It was pleasant to be able to walk about in the open after being cooped up indoors so much, and it was much less cold than it had been. In fact, after scrambling about, she felt warm enough to sit on a fallen tree-trunk in the sun, and survey the scene before her.

Mr. Kirby was standing in front of the sledge to fire, and then sitting down to reload, but Sir Richard remained seated throughout. Jem was squatting on the grass by the horse, apparently deep in conversation with it. Over by the inn, a man was walking a black horse backwards and forwards on the road—Mr. Black, she supposed. The horse was very frisky and frequently broke into a sideways dancing step, trying to break away, and occasionally took a backward kick at the curly-haired stable-lad, who was assisting in some way. The easily-identified forms of Mr. Tupper and Mr. Petts emerged from the little chapel and walked down to the road, then set off along it down the valley.

It was possible from here to form a better idea of the great bulk of Helvellyn, still thickly covered with snow, for it had received the full benefit of the north-westerly wind.

To the right, the road disappeared upwards into a fold in the mountainside, going to Dunmail Raise.

Down the valley, the long lake gleamed dully in the sun, still solidly frozen over. About a mile or so down its length, it suddenly narrowed and appeared to form a strait, with a stone bridge and causeway. Thick clumps of trees covered either promontory, and the roofs and chimneys of two quite large houses could be seen among them. Only one set of chimneys showed any smoke, and not very much even then.

The scene had a certain cold, austere beauty, but Miss Minster found it depressed her spirits and made her feel a deep longing for her own native county. All this seemed so wild and lonely, so empty of life, and yet, even as the thought entered her mind, she heard a faint, shrill whistle, and saw movement on the opposite hillside. A man was moving about up there, and the smaller dark form of a dog could be seen, leaping about in the snow and moving purposefully across the slope. Puzzled, she narrowed her eyes to see better, and eventually picked out the little group of sheep, dirty white against the virgin snow. It must be the old shepherd and his dog at work, she supposed.

Presently, she realised that the shooting had stopped, and when she looked down the slopes, she saw Jem hopping about in the marsh, collecting small, limp bundles, and the two gentlemen dismantling and cleaning their guns. Sir Richard looked up towards her and waved. She waved back, caught up her skirts a little, and ran down the hill to the sledge. It was steeper than she realised, and she arrived with a rush, bonnet fallen back, hair dishevelled, cheeks flushed and eyes bright.

"She was a phantom of delight," Sir Richard remarked in a normal, conversational tone, "When first she gleamed upon my sight; a lovely apparition sent, to be a...er...well, whatever it was."

"A moment's ornament," Miss Minster supplied, with no particular inflexion in her voice, but her eyes met his and held for a little too long. When she turned away to look across the lake and put her bonnet straight, she felt that she understood him very well. Of course, to him she was a momentary amusement, the object of a little light flirtation to while away the time on a tedious journey, and an even more tedious enforced delay in this lonely, dull place. Quite harmless, no doubt, and all to be forgotten once the relief coach came to take them on to their destination. He probably had no idea how much he had disturbed her inner peace, and would be very surprised if he knew how dramatic an effect his kisses had aroused in her. There was really no need for her to worry unduly about it, and certainly no reason for the view in front of her to be so blurred.

"What on earth was that about?" Mr. Kirby enquired of Sir Richard.

"Wordsworth," he replied briefly.

"Who?"

"William Wordsworth."

"Oh. You mean the fellow at Rydal," Mr. Kirby dismissed the literary phenomenon of Lakeland with a marked lack of interest. "We seem to have made a pretty fair bag!" he observed with more interest as Jem returned with his arms full of dead birds.

"I marvel we're not hemmed in three deep by gamekeepers!" Sir Richard replied. "There ain't a breath of wind, and the sound of firing must have carried clear down the valley between these hills!"

Mr. Kirby was helping Jem stack the kill on the sledge, and exclaimed, "Yes, quite good. We could have got three or four times as many, if you hadn't said it was time to stop, though."

"What's the point? There's enough there for a couple of weeks, and they'd not keep longer. I feel like King Herod after the Massacre of the Innocents as it is," Sir Richard said disparagingly. "Pretty little ducks, quacking about in the mud and minding their own business. Seems a shame. I'm a fair shot, but m'heart's not in it. Joe Manton says I lack the instinct of a murderer, which is needed to be a good shooter!"

"That's an odd attitude for a soldier!" Mr. Kirby remarked.

"War ain't sport. Besides, I never really wanted to join the Army. I enjoy the colour and the ceremony, and the skills—training men, turning them from a rabble of gaolbirds to a disciplined force, and so forth, but shooting at a live target, or riding down on infantry and slashing 'em to pieces...such a waste!" He shivered. "I'll be glad when this damned war's over. It's gone on far too long."

"It will not be much longer now, surely?" Miss Minster said quietly, seeing that Mr. Kirby appeared both shocked and embarrassed at such a speech from an officer.

"Another year perhaps. The Russians and Austrians are on the Rhine, and the Beau is in France already, so perhaps even this summer... I'm out of it, at all events."

"Didn't see no 'ares," Jem said regretfully. "Fond of jugged 'are, I am. Still, we got a good few of them black grouses and ducks." Sir Richard caught Miss Minster's eyes, and a spark of amusement passed between them at Jem's disastrous way with plurals as the servant went to fetch the horse.

On the way back to the inn, they met Mr. Black, now mounted on his horse which was going at a brisk trot, still with the occasional attempt to break away. He sketched a cursory salute as he passed, but said nothing, clearly needing all his attention on keeping his mount in hand. Sir

Richard turned to look after him, saying, "That's a hard-mouthed-looking brute! Wouldn't like to keep him in a stall for long—he'd kick it to pieces, I shouldn't wonder!"

"An ill-bred creature," Mr. Kirby observed disdainfully, and Miss Minster wondered if he meant the horse or the rider, then immediately felt a little ashamed of herself for disliking the thief-taker so much.

"'E's bin trying to kick the 'ole stable to flinders these larst two diys!" Jem informed them. "It was get 'im aht or stand clear o' the wreckage, I reckon!"

"By the by," Mr. Kirby said to Miss Minster, smiling upon her with much admiration, for she still had a good colour and more animation than usual, following her walk in the fresh air. "The landlord has found me a couple of pairs of skates, and I'd be happy to give you a little tuition in their use after luncheon, if you would be agreeable."

Miss Minster's face lit up with pleasure at this kind thought and she accepted the offer at once, but Sir Richard said doubtfully, "D'you think the ice is fit? It's a deal warmer today, and the snow's clearly thawing."

"Oh, there's a good thickness on the lake yet," Mr. Kirby replied, brushing the doubt aside. "We'll stay near the shore, where the water is shallow, and the ice thicker. There's no danger."

Sir Richard said nothing, but he still looked unconvinced. However, he was distracted by some uncomfortable lurching as the sledge crossed some hard ruts in the track, no longer filled by snow, and the passengers had to hold on tightly to stay aboard.

The short journey back to the inn was accomplished without mishap, however, and the passengers went indoors, leaving Jem to take the sledge and its burden round to the back.

In the dining-room, they found Mr. Tupper and Mr. Petts returned from their walk, and the latter very busy at the table with a selection of tankards, a couple of bottles of burgundy, sugar and lemon, a nutmeg-grater and a spice-caster, concocting a mixture, while a couple of pokers heated in the fire.

"Mulled wine," he stated as they took off their outdoor clothing. "Receipt by Fred'rick Petts," and proceeded to blend his ingredients in a handsome Queensware jug. Miss Minster watched rather dubiously, feeling that she had consumed an alarming amount of alcohol in the past few days.

Eventually the mixture was to Mr. Petts's liking, despite some helpful suggestions from Mr. Kirby, and he quenched both the pokers in it before filling the tankards. The steaming liquid certainly smelled very good, and a cautious sip confirmed the promise. Miss Minster found it was very pleasant to sit round the fire with the gentlemen and an unobtrusive tuffet of ginger fur, drinking the warming wine and feeling brisk in herself after her jaunt.

Presently, Jem came to collect their coats and hats.

"There's a cove in th' kitchen says as 'ow 'e's a gime-kipper," he said lugubriously.

"Oh dear!" Sir Richard looked more amused than apprehensive. "Is he being—er—troublesome?"

"'E's eating cold beef an' taters," Jem replied. "'E did arsk 'oo'd bin shooting, so I told 'em you was both qualified. 'E said not ter worrit, but would yer kindly consider yerselfs warned orf for the future. I said I fort yer'd be agreeable."

"Damned impertinence," Mr. Kirby murmured, not very loudly.

"Thank you," Sir Richard said, ignoring him. He unbuttoned his coat enough to get at his waistcoat pockets, and produced a coin and a visiting-card. "Give him these, please, in case his master wishes to—er—check my credentials."

"Yer don't need ter give 'im tin. Copper 'ld do!"

"Well, it's Christmas," Sir Richard replied vaguely. "I expect he had a cold walk to get here. I hope he's not eating our luncheon?"

Jem assured him that a Lucullan repast was being prepared for the parlour party—only he termed it "reg'lar bankit"—and before long the maids came to set the table with an adequate array of cold goose, cold beef, ham, cheese, bread, the remains of the veal pie, a dish of eggs, potatoes, cabbage and the jellies and blancmanger untouched from yesterday.

Mr. Black came in late for the meal, limping a little and not in the best of tempers. He offered neither explanation nor apology, and did not make any mention of the muddy patch on the back of his greatcoat, which he pulled off and flung on to the bench under the window, where it promptly slid off on to the floor.

"I'm glad to see you back in one piece," Sir Richard remarked amiably. "That beast of yours looked decidedly cantankerous! I thought you were holding him remarkably well when we met you."

Mr. Black shot him a suspicious look, then, on further consideration, apparently accepted that he had been offered a compliment by one who could claim an expert knowledge of such matters, and admitted to the dish of potatoes that his mount had given him a little trouble through lack of exercise, but had now run it out of its system. He ate hurriedly, and went off as soon as he had finished with a curt, "Excuse me."

After luncheon and a short interval of tea-drinking, Mr. Tupper settled himself for a sleep, Mr. Petts picked up *The*

Bride of Abydos, Mr. Kirby requested Sir Richard to summon Jem and desire him to harness up the sledge again, which he did, and Miss Minster went upstairs to prepare herself for the skating lesson. When she came down, she was surprised to find Sir Richard standing by the sledge as well as Mr. Kirby.

"May as well come and watch, if you've no objection," he said.

Mr. Kirby looked a trifle put out, but made no comment.

They proceeded down to the shore of the lake immediately below the inn, picking a spot far enough from the little beck which tumbled down the ridge a little to the north, and yet not too close to the marshy delta of the streams from the Dunmail end. Sir Richard insisted on Jem trying the ice, which he did by jumping up and down on it several times, without much enthusiasm, muttering that it was always his part to get his feet wet, at which Sir Richard mildly enquired what he thought he was paid for.

The ice appeared perfectly sound, and did not give way or even make ominous noises, so Mr. Kirby assisted Miss Minster to strap the skates over her boots, clasping her ankle, rather unnecessarily, she thought, with one hand while he tugged the straps with the other to see if they were tight enough.

As soon as he was ready himself, he took her hands and helped her to her feet, and then supported her on to the ice with an arm round her waist, and began to skate along slowly himself, guiding her and telling her how best to place her feet. The gliding movement was very pleasant, and she soon gained enough confidence to start skating herself, realising that she was unlikely to fall while he was holding her so firmly.

"Don't go too far out!" Sir Richard called. He was sitting on the sledge watching, the sun, already declining towards the western ridge, reflecting brightly on his helmet.

"He must think I still need a nursemaid!" Mr. Kirby said with some asperity, but he took notice of the warning none the less, and remained close to the shore.

After practising like this for some time, Miss Minster felt she was really making considerable progress, and was not at all nervous when Mr. Kirby lessened his support to no more than a hand on her waist, while he held her hand with his other. Quite soon, she was striking out boldly, and could feel that she was really skating, and not merely being towed along by him.

On shore, Jem stamped his feet and wandered about, or leaned against the horse, and Sir Richard sat hunched in his redingote, prodding the edge of the ice with his stick and watching the skaters from under his helmet with a marked lack of expression. He shifted suddenly and looked as if he was about to stand up when Mr. Kirby moved further from his pupil; steadying her now with only a handclasp.

"There!" he said. "You're virtually doing it alone now!"

Miss Minster felt a momentary apprehension, but nothing disastrous happened, and she managed to stop her own progress as he had shown her, and to turn round without mishap when they had gone a few yards from the shore, and after another ten minutes or so of this, was not even particularly alarmed when Mr. Kirby said, "I'm going to let go your hand now, but there's nothing to fear. If you start to lose your balance, I'll be near enough to catch you."

All went well for some time, and she was beginning to enjoy this new ability, going along with ever-increasing confidence, and then Mr. Kirby turned to call out to Sir

Richard about how well she was progressing, and in doing so, took his attention off her. She was moving parallel to the shore, and had inadvertently gone a little further along than at any time before. The distance between pupil and teacher increased considerably, and then, quite suddenly, she saw something projecting from the ice less than a yard from her feet, and directly in front of her.

She realised that it was part of a submerged treebranch as she struck it with one foot, trying instinctively to lean back and stop herself, and landed heavily on the ice in a sitting position, jarring every bone in her body. There was a curious cracking sound, and she suddenly found herself descending, still sitting, into bitterly cold water, which made her cry out with shock.

Mr. Kirby, turning his attention back to her at the unexpected sound of her fall, darted forward, realised that the ice had given way under her, and braked sharply, falling over himself. Fortunately, he was far enough away from the broken area, and the ice where he landed held firm. Even as he had started to move, however, so had Sir Richard. He flung off his redingote, which was fortunately not buttoned, and went straight to Miss Minster, smashing the remaining ice between her and the shore with his stick and wading out through it to her aid, uttering a most reprehensible phrase when the water reached the tops of his boots and cascaded down inside them.

She had already discovered that the water was only about three feet deep, and was struggling to her feet when he reached her and flung his left arm about her waist, picking her up bodily and crushing her hard against him.

"Put your arms round my neck!" he commanded. "I can't carry you with one arm, but we can manage well enough like this." Obediently, and with great relief, she wrapped her arms about his neck and he struggled back to land with her, half-dragging, half-carrying her and staggering as his injured leg took the additional weight, made greater by her saturated clothes.

Mr. Kirby had recovered his feet, and picked his way gingerly back to dry land, but was unable to make very rapid progress there with his skates on, and Jem had come down to see if he could help, wading a little way into the water—but, prudently, not above his boottops—to receive Miss Minster from his master and carry her to the sledge, Sir Richard limping after them with his knee almost giving way, and an expression of disgust on his face as the water in his boots squelched about uncomfortably.

"Put this round you!" he said, flinging his redingote about Miss Minster and wrapping her in its folds. "Back to the inn, Jem, as fast as you can!"

Mr. Kirby, seeing himself left behind, shouted in protest, but he was ignored and had to unstrap his skates and follow as best he could, while Jem mounted the sledge and urged the horse to a lumbering trot, going up the slope like Boadicea thundering into battle!

Sir Richard tugged at the straps of Miss Minster's skates with one hand, needing the other to hold on to the sledge, scowling ferociously. They were wet and consequently recalcitrant, but he eventually got them loose, and then looked up into her face in concern, for she was making a very odd sound. Then he saw that she was laughing, and a grin appeared on his own face.

"Oh, how ludicrous!" she gasped. "What a ridiculous adventure!"

"Thank God the water was no deeper," he replied, sobering for a moment, and then exploded into laughter himself as he pulled off his boots and emptied them over the side of the sledge.

"It was very good of you to come to the rescue!" she said when they had recovered from their amusement. "I am sure most people would at least have hesitated before plunging into such cold water!"

He shrugged. "I was the nearest. Are you wretchedly cold and uncomfortable?"

She was, exceedingly, but she bravely dismissed it with, "Oh, I can bear it until we reach the inn," at which he put his arm round her and hugged her, as if he was trying to make her feel warmer.

Jem took the sledge straight into the stableyard and up to the kitchen door, and Miss Minster ran as quickly as she could through the kitchen, catching a fleeting impression of open-mouthed scullery-maids, up to their elbows in suds at the two stone sinks, the landlady in a large apron attacking a mountain of dough, two girls peeling potatoes, and a very warm, cheering smell of something very appetising roasting in the brick oven. Sir Richard lingered to explain what had happened while she went straight upstairs to her room and thankfully stripped off her sodden clothing and boots, and towelled herself dry, rubbing briskly with the generous piece of hem-stitched huckaback until her circulation was livened up and spread a warm glow through her limbs.

There was a tap at the door, and the landlady called to her to throw her wet clothes out on the landing, where one of the maids would wait to collect them and take them to be dried and pressed. Miss Minster had been worrying about this, for she had only one redingote and one pair of boots. She quickly bundled the things together, wrapped the towel round her, and opened the door far enough to hand them out to the maid.

By the time she had dressed herself in fresh linen from her trunk and another of her plain day-dresses, she felt much better, and in no danger of taking a chill, and after tidying her hair, went down to the parlour.

Mr. Petts and Mr. Tupper were sitting there, quite wide awake, listening to Mr. Kirby giving them a very dramatic account of the accident, which he broke off as she entered to rush to her side, seize her hand, and exclaim in tones of great anguish, "My dear lady! Heaven be thanked you are safe!" gazing into her face with great emotion, even to the extent of allowing his fine blue eyes to appear decidedly moist.

"Do you not think that perhaps you should retire to bed?" Mr. Tupper enquired anxiously. "I would always advise anyone who had been in danger of taking cold to go to bed *at once*!"

"I think, in fact, there is no danger of anything of the kind," Miss Minster replied firmly. "I am not at all cold now, thanks to Jem bringing me back so quickly. I'm sorry you were left behind, Mr. Kirby."

"Oh, think nothing of it! Of course, he was right to bring you back at once! But what a dreadful thing to happen! If only you had not moved so far away from me! I was quite unable to reach you in time before you fell!" Mr. Kirby fired off a rapid fusillade of exclamations. "I cannot understand how the ice came to break so easily! It seemed so safe and firm! There was no sign of weakness when we tested it! When I fell myself, there was no fracture, and you are such a feather in weight compared with me!"

"There was a tree-branch in the water, with one piece protruding through the ice," Miss Minster explained. "It would no doubt have caused a weakness just there."

"Are you sure?"

"Quite sure. I tripped on it."

While all this was going on, Mr. Petts, without a word, thrust the poker into the fire and then left the room, and now returned with the ingredients necessary for Hot Tiger, which he proceeded swiftly to prepare, handing Miss Minster a tankard-full as soon as it was ready. She thanked him with a smile and drank it gratefully, thinking that if he was a highwayman, he was certainly a kindly and practical one. The hot mixture drove out the last vestiges of cold and shock from her system.

"Ah, there you are!" Sir Richard exclaimed, coming into the room, apparently having changed his boots and trousers, although it was difficult to be sure as those he was wearing were identical to the ones he had worn before. "Are you recovered? I was afraid you might be laid out in a dead faint somewhere."

"I am not given to fainting," she replied. "I trust you changed out of your wet clothes?"

"Yes. Couldn't squelch about in those boots a moment longer—I'll swear they felt as if they were full of tadpoles!"

"Not at this time of year!" Mr. Tupper pointed out.

"What the devil were you doing to let Dorcas move out of your reach?" Sir Richard demanded of Mr. Kirby. "You said you'd be near enough to support her if she lost her balance!"

"I hadn't realised that Miss Minster was moving so quickly," Mr. Kirby replied stiffly. "I might have reached her in time if you had not distracted me by talking to me!" It looked for a moment as if there might be some unpleasantness, but Mr. Petts moved smartly between the two gentlemen, who were glaring like fighting-cocks, and thrust a tankard of Hot Tiger into Sir Richard's hand, successfully diverting him.

"Oh, thank you," he said, disconcerted. "That's very thoughtful of you! Just the thing!"

"It wasn't anyone's fault," Miss Minster said, sitting down by the table. "I should have been quite all right if there had not happened to be that branch sticking out of the ice. I didn't see it until it was too late to avoid it, and then it tripped me, and it must have weakened the ice just there."

"I hope this won't give you a misliking for skating?" Mr. Kirby pulled a chair to her and sat down on it.

"No. It was very pleasant. I shall try again, if ever I have the opportunity. Thank you for teaching me."

Sir Richard took his usual chair, and Mr. Tupper and Mr. Petts sat side by side on the settle, and there was a slightly constrained silence for a few minutes, and then Sir Richard said, "I wonder if the relief coach will come tomorrow. The snow seems to be thawing quite well now."

"Yes. Did you notice the clouds building up in the south?" Mr. Kirby offered, apparently accepting Sir Richard's conversational gambit as an olive branch.

"Oh dear! I hope that doesn't mean more snow!" Miss Minster said anxiously.

"Not from the south," Mr. Kirby reassured her, with his very charming smile. "They will bring rain, and very soon, at that!"

As if to confirm his forecast, Jem came in with the candles, for the early winter dusk was already upon them, and said gloomily, "It's just starting to rine cats and dogs! Mr. Black's aht in it, and 'e'll get soaked, and the kitchen's full o' wet clo'es awready!"

But Mr. Black did not get soaked. He came in a few minutes later, having apparently been in the stables grooming his horse, for he remarked in quite a friendly fashion to Mr. Kirby that the latter's mare looked in much better fettle and was standing quite well on her strained leg, which sent Mr. Kirby to see for himself, as he said that she had not been putting any weight on it when he looked at her before luncheon.

"I must take a look at this remarkable animal!" Sir Richard commented lazily, settling back in his chair and obviously having no intention of going out to a cold and draughty stable. "She appears to be the apple of Kirby's eye, and a piece of horseflesh unparalleled since Bucephalus parted this life!"

"Bew—what?" Mr. Black enquired, looking puzzled. "Thought I knew every champion 'orse since the Byerley Turk, but I ain't 'eard o' that one!"

"Ah, but he was a war-horse, not a race-horse!" Miss Minster replied, as Sir Richard seemed to be having some difficulty in articulating.

CHAPTER NINE

BY THE TIME they had eaten dinner, the rain had slackened its first onslaught to a steady fall of more reasonable proportions, and a glance out of the window showed that it was removing the last of the snow from the valley and some way up the ridges on either side. It gurgled in the drain-pipes and swelled the little cascade by the chapel into a sizeable waterfall.

After dinner, the company split in the customary way, Mr. Petts and Mr. Black going to the tap-room, Mr. Kirby to the stables to supervise Jem while he applied a fresh poultice to the precious mare, and the others to the parlour. They were soon joined by the cat Maurice, who thumped at the door until Mr. Tupper got up and let it in. It then climbed on to Sir Richard's lap forthwith and watched with interest as its friend played a game or two of thumpers with Miss Minster.

Presently, Mr. Kirby returned and announced that his mare was certainly much better, a piece of news which he clearly felt should rejoice the hearts of his audience and revive their spirits considerably, but he had decided that, if the relief coach arrived in the morning, he would travel on it to Keswick, as he had urgent business to attend, and return for his horse later, being confident that the landlord would take good care of the precious animal.

"Besides," he added, "I shall then have the great pleasure of your company a little longer, and may, in fact, have something of interest to tell you when we arrive there!''

This appeared to be addressed to Miss Minster—at least, he was looking at her when he said it, but she assumed it to be no more than a general remark and took no notice, missing the significant look at her which accompanied the words. Sir Richard, on the other hand, noticed, and gave the young man rather a sharp glance, and then appeared to fall into a very lengthy consideration of his next move in the current game of thumpers.

Miss Minster retired fairly early, feeling a little worn after her afternoon adventure, and found herself lying awake, listening to the rain and thinking with growing dread of continuing her journey in the morning.

Obviously, she could not hope to stay at the Nag's Head for ever, but during the curious hiatus of these last few days, she had come to regard the little inn with affection, as a place of warm friendliness, unlike the atmosphere in which she had lived since her father's death. Here, she had been able to resume her proper place in Society, as a baronet's daughter, at least as far as most of her companions were concerned, but, however kind the Partridges might be—and she was very much afraid that they would not be kind at all, for Sir Marmaduke's curt letter was not encouraging—in their household, she would again be a mere governess.

Besides, going on to Cockermouth would mean parting from her new friends—from fussy, kindly Mr. Tupper, from dour Mr. Petts, who might be a highwayman, but was really quite a pleasant man under that silent exterior—from Jem and his devastating way with the English language, from handsome Mr. Kirby and his flattering attention, which made her feel like the attractive young lady she might have been if—if things had been different.

She was reluctant to form the last name, even in her mind. Richard. Would she ever again meet someone who would call her "M'dear", or even "Dorcas", and stir her senses as he had done? Already, she was beginning to think of him in the past tense, and by this time tomorrow night, she would most probably have seen the last of him...

He had said he would write her, but that was surely just an idle remark—something to say? He would stay with his sister for a few weeks, and then return to his own home, far away in Hampshire, and forget all about the plain, dowdy little governess at the Nag's Head. Indeed, by the time he left Cumberland, he would quite probably be engaged to marry one of those young ladies whom his sister had invited to meet him.

It was really very foolish to feel so low and wretched— the shock of falling through the ice must have been greater than she had realised, for what else could be making her throat ache in this painful way, and her eyes fill with tears which spilled over and ran down her face as fast as she wiped them away...

By morning, the rain had stopped and the clouds were gradually giving way to a little dubious sunshine. The maid who came to light the fire in Miss Minster's room and bring her hot water, also brought her clothes, dried, brushed and beautifully pressed, and her boots, a little stiff, but quite dry and wearable.

Miss Minster thanked her and asked who had done the work, and when the maid admitted shyly that she had done it herself, gave her three shillings in token of her gratitude.

After the girl had gone, she emptied her stockingpurse on the patch-work quilt and counted her remaining money. Nine shillings and threepence! She must give at least two shillings apiece to the driver and guard of the cross-mail, and what if she had to dine or stay the night in Cockermouth? Clearly, she would have to accept Sir Richard's offer to pay her reckoning here, which would surely be a great deal more than nine shillings! She hated the thought of falling into debt, but there was no alternative now. "Besides," a comforting little voice in her head pointed out, "If you owe him money, at least he will remember you exist, until you've paid it back, at any rate!"

But how could she pay it back? She would have virtually no money at all until June, and then have to practise the strictest economy until December—a whole year! It was a dismal prospect, but there was nothing to be done to improve it, so there was no use in brooding over it. She pushed her purse back into the reticule and set about washing and dressing and repacked her trunk. It did not occur to her to investigate what else might be in the reticule, for she still had no notion that Sir Richard had hidden those three guineas in it on Christmas Day.

The relief coach eventually appeared as they were gathered in expectation of luncheon, after waiting about all the morning wondering if it would come. It drew up to a jingling halt before the inn, the spare horse which the guard had hired from the landlord tied on at the back, and their old acquaintance, the guard, came in soon after, accompanied by a stout, red-faced fellow in the usual dragsman's surtout and white beaver, who stood in the doorway and beamed upon them all indiscriminately while the guard, now restored to his usual careful mode of speech, bade them, "Good morning."

"Good morning to you, and we're all very pleased to see you safe and well!" Sir Richard replied amongst the others' murmured greetings. "Did you have a very bad time after you left us?"

The guard looked distinctly taken aback at hearing a passenger actually enquire after his well-being, but he soon recovered enough to thank Sir Richard and assure him that his journey had only been middling uncomfortable, compared with some he had known, and that he arrived in Cockermouth during the morning of Christmas Eve, only fourteen hours late.

"And I trust you are not to be fined for it?" Sir Richard pursued.

The guard cast an eloquent glance upon Mr. Tupper, who looked out of the window rather self-consciously, and replied that he believed not, but would not know for certain until his written report had been seen by the Postmaster-General.

Sir Richard handed him one of his visiting cards and bade him write to the Hampshire address if he found the Postmaster-General unsympathetic. Mr. Tupper took the hint, and produced a card of his own, saying in a low, agitated voice, "Oh, no! You must call on me, for indeed it was my fault the horses ran away, I freely admit!"

"Very kind, much appreciated, gentlemen!" the guard assured them, placing both cards in some secure inner recess of his many layers of clothing. "Now, I dare say you are anxious to proceed, and as soon as t'horses are baited and coachman and I have eaten a bite, we'll be on our way. Shall we say forty-five minutes, if you please?"

At this point, he caught sight of Mr. Black and Mr. Kirby, and said, "Nay, then! You two gentlemen ain't my passengers!"

"No," replied Mr. Black. "I goes me own way on me own four legs, thankee!"

"But I'll be glad to join you, if you've room," Mr. Kirby put in.

The guard agreed cautiously that room might be found, and accepted Mr. Kirby's fare at once, for he proffered the full amount from Kendal, and graciously told the guard to keep the change!

As the guard and driver withdrew, Jem replaced them in the doorway and said he would see their traps safely stowed in the basket, and send the landlord to settle their reckoning. Miss Minster decided to run upstairs again to make sure her trunk was properly locked, thinking as she did so that she was fast falling into the habit common among those with few possessions of being particularly anxious to retain what little they had. While she was above-stairs, she collected her outdoor clothing to save time later, and after a painful hesitation, left another shilling on the tallboy for the chambermaid.

When she returned to the dining-room, she found the others settling up with the landlord, who turned to her as she entered, tendering a folded piece of paper, obviously her bill. Before she could take it, Sir Richard intercepted it and included it with his own, smilingly waving away Mr. Tupper's whispered enquiry, and handing over an assortment of coins to the landlord, adding no less than two sovereigns for vails, trusting that he would distribute the money among the servants as he thought they deserved. The landlord protested that it was too much, but Sir Richard pointed out that it was for three guests, including Jem, and that he believed in rewarding good service, at which the landlord thanked him very much and withdrew backwards, bowing, as from the presence of Royalty, inadvertently admitting the cat Maurice as he did so.

The animal made for the fireplace, and established himself on the rag rug with the air of one who intends a lengthy stay. Miss Minster attempted to thank Sir Richard and ascertain how much she owed him, but he replied smilingly, "We'll talk about it later."

Mr. Kirby had observed his interception of Miss Minster's bill, and approached Sir Richard with a puzzled frown at the first opportunity, and said discreetly, "I thought you said she ain't under your protection?"

Sir Richard gave him a searching look and replied with equal discretion, "So I did, and I assure you it's true. You need have no fears about that! She's had the misfortune to run short of the necessary, her new employer not having sent her fare, and I'm lending her a little. Nothing underhand, I give you my word!"

Mr. Kirby looked relieved. "I just wanted to be sure," he said, then added self-consciously, "I *have* to be sure!"

"I thought you might," Sir Richard replied, looking at him in an oddly melancholy fashion. "Good luck!" and with that, he moved away to his place at table, as luncheon was just arriving.

The meal was eaten without much conversation as time was short, and they were all engaged in adjusting their minds to a return to normal life after this interval in a snow-bound limbo. As the last slices of mince tart and crumbs of cheese were being consumed, Mr. Black got up and sauntered over to the window.

Miss Minster glanced that way to see what he was about, and caught sight of the stable-lad walking Mr. Black's horse to and fro in the forecourt, near to the presently horse-less coach. The thief-taker exchanged a nod with the boy, picked up his greatcoat from the window-seat and put it on, then strolled unhurriedly to the door. He was now behind Miss Minster, and she did not see him turn the key in the lock and set his back against the door, a double-barreled holster-pistol in his right hand.

"Now then!" he said loudly and briskly, cutting across some remark Mr. Kirby was making. "I'm not playing games with this popper what you sees in me 'and! It's loaded, and I'm a crack shot. All of you, stand up, quiet and slow-like, and move away from the table!"

There was a startled silence as they all stared at him, and he jerked the pistol meaningly with a sharp "Move!" They rose to their feet and obediently backed away from the table, Mr. Kirby going towards the window, where he collided with Mr. Petts, and in the confusion, the latter moved round closer to Black, but was discouraged by finding the two evil black circles at the ends of the pistol-barrels pointing in his direction. He stopped, and Mr. Kirby retreated almost to the window-seat.

Mr. Tupper stepped back on the rag rug, where he trod on the cat's tail and was nearly frightened into a fit by the snarl and sharp bite in the ankle which drew his attention to his misdemeanour. He was so shaken by events that he murmured an apology, which Maurice apparently accepted as he composed himself to sleep again, ignoring the odd behaviour of the humans.

Sir Richard moved a little towards Black, apparently only to draw Miss Minster out of the line of fire, but the result placed him effectively between her and the pistol, and a good yard nearer Black than his original position.

"Now, without doing anything foolish," Black continued, "One by one, as I tells you, put your waluables on the bread platter in the middle of the table. You first, Mr. Pad-borrower!"

Mr. Petts advanced to the table, and with rather elaborate carefulness, removed his money and his watch from his pockets, placed them on the platter and retired, once more trying to move nearer to Black, but was brusquely ordered away with a menacing little flick of the pistol.

"Now the puzzle-cove."

Mr. Tupper, looking exceedingly frightened and worried, hastily ransacked his pockets and put money and watch with Mr. Petts's property, then returned to the rug, looking round nervously to be sure of avoiding the cat's tail.

"Now Adonis," making a sardonic insult of it. Mr. Kirby started, not realising that Black was referring to him until the movement of the pistol made it clear. Miss Minster was surprised by the classical allusion, not realising that the name had a slightly scurrilous cant meaning.

"Really!" Mr. Kirby protested, hastening to add his contribution to the growing pile. "It's very mean-spirited of you to rob people when you've sat at table with them!"

Black gave a snort of amusement. "I ain't a pretty-mannered fellow like you, me cully! Back to your corner!" as Mr. Kirby seemed disposed to linger by the table.

"Now you, me lord Squire!"

Sir Richard turned and limped to the table, contriving to give Miss Minster a comforting smile on the way, and cast a handful of coins on to the pile with a disdainful gesture.

"Would you like my stick and sabre as well?" he enquired in a drily sarcastic tone. "The stick has a silver knob, and the sabre was a hundred-guinea presentation."

"No. Too awkward to carry. I'll 'ave your ticking-cheat."

"I don't carry a watch."

"'Ookey Walker! Don't waste my time!"

"It's the truth," Sir Richard replied. "Mine caught a bullet at Salamanca, and I've not replaced it yet."

Black still looked disbelieving, but he let the matter drop, waved Sir Richard away from the table, and pulled a cloth bag from his pocket with his left hand.

"Now, me pretty!" to Miss Minster. "Come over 'ere!"

Miss Minster reluctantly walked over to him. She did not feel particularly frightened, for the whole scene still appeared unreal to her, as if she was watching a play at the theatre.

"Put the blunt and tickers in 'ere, not forgetting your own little contribution, and bring it back to me!"

"Claude Duval never robbed a lady!" Mr. Petts said meaningly.

"'E got 'anged just the same!" Black pointed out.

Miss Minster took the bag and went to the table. With some vague idea that delaying matters might give time for something to happen, she fumbled clumsily as she collected the coins and watches and put them in the bag, then opened her reticule, took out her purse, had some pretended difficulty in opening it, and added her own few coins, one by one.

"Sharp's the word!" Black exclaimed. "I got urgent business elsewhere!"

Miss Minster returned to him with the bag and contrived to drop it as she handed it to him, wincing at the thought of the watches striking the stone floor.

"Now pick it up!" he snarled, and menaced her with the pistol, at which Sir Richard took a step forward. Instantly, the pistol was pointed at him as Miss Minster stooped to retrieve the bag. Black snatched it from her and stuffed it into the pocket of his coat.

"Now, Miss 'Igh-and-mighty! Turn your back to me!" She obeyed, and was seized and dragged back hard against Black's chest, his left arm clamped across her, pinning her arms to her sides above the elbows, and feeling like an iron bar across her breasts. The hand holding the pistol was clearly visible to her at the level of her waist and projecting the length of Black's lower arm in front of her. She saw that it was still pointing at Sir Richard, who had taken another step forward as he made a sound of protest at Black's roughness.

"Listen carefully, all of you!" Black said. "I'm leaving 'ere now, and the mort comes with me! She's me 'ostage, so if anyone interferes in any way, she gets a bullet through 'er! Understand?"

"There's really no call for all this high drama!" Sir Richard said mildly. "Miss Minster can't go off with you without so much as a coat in this season of the year! If you must take a hostage, I'll go with you. There's no need to put the lady to any inconvenience." He had unobtrusively moved closer as he was speaking.

"Think you're very downy, don't you?" Black jeered. "I ain't slowing my pad with your weight! I'm taking the doxy 'cause she's the lightest, not 'cause I wants 'er! I'll drop 'er off a few miles down the road, and you'll get 'er back safe enough, if nobody makes no trouble!"

"You really expect a lady to walk a 'few miles' in this wild country, alone, and without coat or bonnet? Be reasonable man! There's no call for it! If you won't take me instead, then take my word that there'll be no pursuit! We'll let you get away, without doing anything to prevent you." At each sentence, Sir Richard took another slow step forward, apparently unconsciously, and Black did not appear to notice, being too amused at the gentleman's concern for the lady, and his naivety in thinking his word sufficient to secure her release.

"You can go on your knees and beg me, if you like!" he said sardonically.

Miss Minster, frozen with horror now at Sir Richard's slow approach to what might well be his own immediate demise, stared at him, willing him to stop, to retreat. She saw a muscle tighten and twitch by his mouth at the jibe, but he took yet another step forward as he replied, "Well, I'll try if it helps matters, but, quite honestly, I doubt if I can manage it." Miss Minster moved her right foot a fraction and located one of Black's boots.

"It won't 'elp you nothing if you comes another step nearer!" Black said unpleasantly. "I can see what you're up to, me cully, so just back off a little, or I'll put a bullet through your other knee!"

Sir Richard was now about six feet from the muzzles of the pistol. He stopped and stood still for a moment, apparently considering Black's threat. Miss Minster forced her eyes from his face and looked down at Black's hand. She saw his finger tighten perceptibly on one trigger. Without hesitation, she shouted "Richard!" at the top of her voice and stamped as hard as she could on Black's foot. A fraction later, Sir Richard lunged forward, his stick swinging up to catch Black a sharp crack on the right wrist, falling himself as his knees gave way and twisting sideways as he went down.

The pistol went off with a surprisingly loud bang. The portrait of King George over the fireplace crashed down on the hearth, narrowly missing the cat Maurice, which sprang in the air with a yowl of fright and landed four-square on Mr. Tupper's waist-coat. The solicitor's arms closed round the animal in a reflex action as he stepped back, tripped on the rug, and sat down abruptly on the floor, where he prudently decided to remain.

Miss Minster tore herself loose from Black's grip as it slackened in surprise and flung herself on top of Sir Richard to protect his defenceless back from the second bullet, but Black's hand was temporarily numbed by Sir Richard's blow, and before he could transfer the weapon to his other hand, Mr. Petts sprang on him and knocked it away. It skidded across the floor, and Sir Richard stretched out a hand and neatly fielded it as it passed him.

Mr. Petts wrestled with Black, and Mr. Kirby went to his aid, and then there was a loud, metallic snap, followed within seconds by another, and Black suddenly stood still, staring in disbelief at the manacles fast round his wrists. The fight had gone out of him completely.

"Oh, I say! Well done!" exclaimed Mr. Kirby admiringly.

Mr. Petts twitched his nose in a satisfied sniff and recited rapidly, "By wirtue of the authority wested in me, Fred'rick Petts, by the magistrates of Bow Street Court in the County of Middlesex, I arrests you, 'Enery Black, alias Black Beelzebub, for 'ighway robbery, grand and compound larceny, attempted murder, and attempted habduction!"

"Ah!" said Sir Richard in tones of great interest, "So *you're* the Bow Street Runner! No wonder you were certain he wasn't!"

Sounds of activity from outside the door heralded the approach of others, attracted by the shot. Mr. Petts unlocked the door, and was almost knocked over by Jem, who dashed in and exclaimed "Oh, my Gawd!" at the sight of his master and Miss Minster prostrate on the floor in a heap.

"Jem!" exclaimed Sir Richard irately.

"Yes sir! Sorry sir! Sorry Miss! Sorry all! 'Ere, are you orlright sir? We 'eard a shot!"

Miss Minster sat up, feeling foolish, and allowed Sir Richard to roll over and sit up too. He promptly put an arm round her shoulders and replied to Jem, "I think you'll find our unfortunate monarch provided the target—unintentionally, I'm sure, for I'd not wish to add High Treason to that imposing list of charges!"

Mr. Kirby started forward to assist Miss Minster to rise, but she pointed past him and exclaimed, "The stable-boy!"

Mr. Petts ran to the window and caught a glimpse of the boy vaulting into the saddle of Black's horse, then swung round and made for the door, exclaiming "Stop 'im!" Unfortunately, the landlord, the guard and the coachman were standing in a group in the doorway or just inside it, looking about for the expected carnage, and there was a considerable entanglement as they tried to get out of the way and only succeeded in blocking it completely for a few vital seconds. Before Mr. Petts could break through, they heard the sound of hooves pounding along the road towards Keswick.

"Hell-and-damnation-sorry-Miss!" Mr. Petts exclaimed, almost as one word. "'E'll be orf to warn the rest of the gang! Oh well, too late now. 'Ere, where's Tupper?"

Mr. Tupper and the cat Maurice were discovered sitting on the hearth-rug, still close in embrace, and there was a general move to pick them up and sort them out. Miss Minster, feeling a trifle overcome, was much inclined to rest her head on Sir Richard's shoulder, and perhaps indulge in a few tears, but before she could do so, Mr. Kirby carried out his deferred intention and seized her hand, helped her solicitously to her feet, and said, "My dear lady! Such courage! Such presence of mind! Oh, what a dreadful risk! You should not have endangered your precious life in such a hazardous enterprise! If the surprise had not succeeded! If Sir Richard had not been near enough to strike away that gun! He might have *injured* you!''

"But he would certainly have shot Sir Richard!" Miss Minster pointed out, wishing he would not gush in such a sentimental fashion, although she was quite glad to sink down on the chair to which he guided her.

"I'm quite sure Sir Richard would have preferred you not to have taken such a risk!" said Mr. Kirby with conviction.

"Sir Richard would most certainly *not* have preferred to be shot!" that gentleman declared positively from where he was still sitting on the floor, unloading the remaining ball from Black's pistol.

"Sir Richard ain't a fool or a martyr, you know! I've had enough of getting in the way of odd bullets, and I can assure you, I don't care for it at all! I'm much obliged to D- to Miss Minster for her very competent action, and I'd be obliged to you, Mr. Kirby if you'd stop talking nonsense and give me a hand up. This floor is damned hard!''

Mr. Kirby hastened to his assistance, but was forestalled by Jem, who had the knack required, and when he was up, Sir Richard added, "And of course, m'dear, I'm very sorry you were put to the necessity of taking a risk yourself!''

"I didn't wish him to shoot you!" she replied with reasonable calm. "Why ever did you try to stop him? You might have been killed!" she added, with much more agitation.

"I wasn't going to allow him to put you to the inconvenience of being carried off by him," Sir Richard explained. "Besides, he annoyed me, doubting m'word—damned impudence!"

Mr. Petts meanwhile had relieved his prisoner of the bag of loot and had fished his watch out of it, held it to his ear, and allowed himself a small whistle of relief at finding it still to be working.

"If you're on your feet again," he said to Mr. Tupper, "Per'aps you'll return this 'ere to its rightful owners."

"Yes. Yes. Oh, dear!" Mr. Tupper looked about him for somewhere to put the cat Maurice, which was still clutched to his waistcoat, and then handed it to Jem, who entered into a soothing conversation with the still-indignant animal. The solicitor took the bag and invited Miss Minster to reclaim her property.

Sir Richard and Mr. Kirby then took theirs, Mr. Tupper removed his own money and watch, and returned the bag to Mr. Petts, who counted the remaining coins and put them in his pocket.

"All *h*onest folk 'ere!" he remarked, with a withering look at the notably dishonest one, who was still standing with bent head, apparently contemplating his manacles.

"I think a round of brandy would not come amiss," Sir Richard suggested to the landlord, who went off to fetch it. "And then I think we'd best be on our way, if we're to reach Cockermouth before nightfall!"

"I'm afraid you'll not do that, in any case." Mr. Petts observed gloomily. "I shall 'ave to require your assistance to conwey my prisoner to the lockup in Keswick, and then all of you to swear an affydavy about the goings-on 'ere!"

"Affidavit," Mr. Tupper corrected automatically. "Yes, Mr. Petts is quite right! We shall have to do that of course, or else find ourselves summoned to the next Assizes, which may not be at all convenient! Fortunately, I am acquainted with the Commissioner of Oaths in Keswick, and that should expedite matters!'' Mr. Tupper noticed the remains of the king's portrait at this point, and exclaimed, ''Oh dear! The frame seems quite beyond repair! What a pity—such a good print!''

''I'll send you a new picture of the King from London when I return there,'' Sir Richard said to the landlord as he paid him for the brandy, for which he expressed much gratitude. He then collected the cat from Jem in order to remove it to the kitchen, and seemed quite touched when Sir Richard shook its paw and bade it farewell as it was borne past him. The cat blinked slowly in a feline smile, and then climbed up to adopt its favourite position round the landlord's neck, and so made its departure from the scene.

CHAPTER TEN

WHILE THE TRAVELLERS were drinking their brandy—and Miss Minster was startled to see that Black had been served with a glass as well—Mr. Petts informed the guard that he would have to require a passage for his prisoner to Keswick, but would accompany him Outside, not wishing to inflict a criminal presence on the other passengers. This caused a little bureaucratic flurry as Mr. Petts had already paid inside fare, and Black, of course, was not on the way-bill at all. This problem was solved by the guard returning a shilling to Mr. Petts, and then receiving it back again in settlement of Black's fare.

The guard was then seized with an unpleasant thought, and enquired anxiously if Mr. Petts thought there might be any trouble on the road.

"Not from 'im," Mr. Petts replied, indicating his prisoner. "But we might run into some of 'is friends, if that was where that boy was orf to."

"I'm sure we can deal with any problems of that nature, between us," Sir Richard said. "I've a pair of pistols, as well as my shotguns, Mr. Kirby has his Wogans, the guard, I suppose, has a blunderbuss, and there's Black's pistol, apart from whatever artillery you carry yourself, Mr. Petts. Jem shall have my shotguns, and he and I will contrive to manage from the windows, and the rest of you can join in from the roof. Miss Minster and Mr. Tupper will travel inside, of course."

Mr. Kirby was a little slow to realise that this business-like plan would place him outside, but as he opened his mouth to protest, he realised that only one person could hope to use each window as a fire-port, that Sir Richard obviously could not climb on the roof, that if he insisted on going inside, it would look as if he wanted a safer place and was prepared to put Jem into danger to get it, and so shut his mouth again. Sir Richard, making a good guess at his thoughts from the changing expressions flitting across his face, allowed himself a slight sardonic smile.

After that, they wasted no more time, but bade farewell to the landlord, his wife and the servants, hoisted the original driver on to the box beside his relief, and Miss Minster, Sir Richard and Mr. Tupper took their former positions inside, Jem moving into Mr. Petts's corner. The others climbed on the roof and Black was secured to the rail running round the edge by a second pair of hand-cuffs threaded through the seat about his wrists. The blankets were removed from the team, the guard tootled a salute, and off they set, springing to a brisk trot along the length of Leatheswater.

The snow had almost completely vanished from the valley, except for a few wreaths caught in the uneven-nesses of the ground, but the fells above them still carried a blanket of white which gleamed in the hazy sun. The ice had broken up on the lake, and there were large numbers of waterfowl on the surface.

The travelling-rug was lying on the seat by Sir Richard, who picked it up, unfolded it, and leaned forward to spread it over Miss Minster, who accepted the kindness with a smile. He smiled back, but only briefly, and then transferred his attention to the view from the window, leaving her with a sad feeling which she found difficult to analyse—disappointment? Rejection?

"Funny fing, Mr. Petts turning aht ter be a Scarlet Runner!" Jem commented.

"Even funnier, Black pretending to be one!" Sir Richard replied. "He really made a mistake there—virtually asking Petts to suspect him."

"It was very confusing," Miss Minster said. "Mr. Petts always seemed a pleasant man, if rather terse, but we thought him a villain, and Mr. Black was always unpleasant, yet claimed to be a Bow Street Runner! I don't believe I've ever met a Runner before, so I had no idea how to expect one to be."

She only half-heard Mr. Tupper's little lecture which followed this, and gradually wandered off into her own rather melancholy train of thought as he discoursed on the qualifications needed to be a thief-taker, going on to a brief history of the Bow Street Runners and their co-founders, John and Henry Fielding, the former magistrates.

"There's a buzzard up there!" Sir Richard observed, breaking the interval of silence which followed Mr. Tupper's eventual running-down. "Do you see it?" Miss Minster started, and obediently pressed close to the window, twisting to follow the line indicated by his pointing finger, and caught a brief glimpse of a large bird hovering above the slopes of Helvellyn. "Looking for rabbits, I expect," he added.

"So long as 'e don't take me for one!" Jem commented.

"I don't think they eat hedgehogs," his master replied kindly, and so echoed Miss Minster's thought that she laughed. Sir Richard was seized with a sharp attack of coughing, and Jem sniffed in indignant disgust.

After a few miles, the road swung away from the lake, and presently the coach slowed and then drew up before the regular post-house. The relief driver and the guard got down and went into conference about whether or not to take on a fresh team as the old one had only covered eight miles since the last change, and had been baited for an hour in the middle of it.

"I wouldn't presume to tell you your business," Sir Richard said diffidently, having pulled down the window and put his head out to hear what they were saying, "But I've an idea we may be glad of a fresh team before we reach Keswick."

"Ay, you're reet," the guard replied. "We'll have a change."

Mr. Petts could be heard lending his support to this, and the coachman, who had not considered it necessary, shrugged indifferently, as it was not his responsibility in any case. The team was changed, Sir Richard closed the window, and they started off again.

As he settled himself back in his corner, Sir Richard caught sight of the serious look on Miss Minster's face, and enquired, "I hope the talk of an attack ain't alarmed you? You look very worried. It probably won't happen—we're just taking precautions in case."

"I wasn't thinking about that," she replied.

"What, then?"

"Oh—wondering what I shall find when I arrive at my destination. About the future generally, I suppose."

"You may find there's nothing to worry about after all," he said, choosing his words carefully so that they might offer a little hope and comfort without being too specific, in case his ideas about Mr. Kirby's intentions proved wrong. "And if, in the end, you find it's as bad as you feared, don't forget to write to me, and I'll set about finding you something better."

"Would you really?" Her expression brightened, for he had now repeated the offer, and this made her feel that perhaps he really meant it.

"I'm sure I could contrive to find a pleasant family somewhere amongst my acquaintance who have need of a governess, or I may be able to offer something better— if you need it, of course. As I said, you may find everything has turned out as right as ninepence by tomorrow!"

"'Ow many did you siy was in Black Beaslybub's gang?" Jem asked Mr. Tupper, who automatically corrected the pronunciation of the name before replying, "I believe there are usually two, but I would not be prepared to swear to it, for reports differ and may be exaggerated."

"One couldn't exaggerate very much and still arrive at a sum total of two!" Sir Richard pointed out, deliberately catching Jem's eye and shaking his head slightly, indicating with a complicated wriggle of his eyebrows that the subject might alarm Miss Minster.

Leatheswater came to an end, and the road turned away from the valley. A round, pudding-shaped hill arose on their left, and they began to climb uphill towards the shoulder of High Rigg. Another half-mile along the road, a rough track branched off to the right, past a toll-house, rising steeply to pass below what looked at first like a ruined castle. Miss Minster looked at it with interest for a few minutes, and then realised that in fact it was a natural formation. The track passed very close to its base, going into the narrow pass which it appeared to guard, presumably into another valley.

Just as she was about to turn her eyes away from it, a sudden movement on the track caught her attention. Two riders had just come over the ridge and were moving at a fast trot down the hill towards the tollgate. One of them flung up an arm to point at the coach, and they both urged their mounts to a gallop.

"Look!" she exclaimed.

Sir Richard looked, said, "Here comes trouble!" in a resigned tone, and pulled down the window to shout a warning to the guard, who shouted back that he had already seen them.

Miss Minster found herself watching with interest to see if the riders would stop to pay before coming on to the turnpike, but she was unable to see as the road was turning to the left to take the steeper part of the pass they were entering at an angle. The coachman began cracking his whip and shouting "Ha!" rather ineffectually, as the road was climbing more and more steeply, and the cattle could not take it at more than a walk.

"Better get the boxes out," Sir Richard told Jem, who got down in the straw and pulled two flattish wooden cases from under the seat. The larger one Miss Minster recognised as the case of Sir Richard's sporting guns. The other proved to contain a pair of double-barrelled holster-pistols, very plain and workmanlike, with blued metal and polished about the butts as if they had seen much use.

"You take the shotguns, Jem!" Sir Richard instructed, starting to load the pistols.

"Fair enough," Jem replied, setting to work to assemble and load them. "You're a better shot nor me. Can yer manage left-'anded?"

Miss Minster wondered why Sir Richard should have to shoot left-handed, and then realised that it was because he was on the off-side of the coach and would be firing to the rear.

"I shall contrive to do so," he replied, emptying ready-prepared charges down the barrel of one pistol, and wrapping the cartridge paper round the balls before ramming them after it. "Old guns, these—belonged to m'father," he informed Miss Minster conversationally, "but very reliable." He made a small adjustment to the setting of the flint in the swan-necked cock, laid the pistol aside, and started on its partner.

There was a sudden odd sound, not unlike a hornet, which stopped with an abrupt rap on the window-frame. A few splinters of wood sprayed out and the glass cracked across. An almighty roaring bang sounded from the roof a second later.

"They appear to be within range," Sir Richard remarked coolly, seeing Miss Minster's startled expression. "The crack of doom was the guard's blunderbuss. He'd have done better to hold his fire—it has a very short range. I think, m'dear girl, you'd better sit on the floor, if you wouldn't mind. It don't appear too dirty."

Miss Minster slipped off the seat and made herself reasonably comfortable in the straw on the floor in the middle of the coach, while Sir Richard pulled down the window and cautiously looked out. Another hornet whined past, which made him raise his eyebrows a trifle, and then he pressed his face against the window-frame and squinted along the side of the coach at an acute angle.

There was a sudden double report from Jem's side of the vehicle, and Mr. Tupper let out a squeak of mingled alarm and excitement, then prudently joined Miss Minster on the floor.

"Any luck?" enquired Sir Richard.

"Nah. Missed 'im!" Jem replied, reloading.

The speed of the coach suddenly began to increase as they reached the top of the rise and began to descend towards Naddale. The coachman could be heard springing the horses to a trot, then a canter, and eventually a full gallop. The coach, which was not designed for such treatment, swayed madly from side to side, lurching and jolting on the uneven road, and Mr. Tupper cried "We'll be over in a minute!" in tones of acute alarm. Miss Minster drew her knees up to her chin and clasped her arms round them, and Sir Richard found time to reach down and give her an encouraging pat on the shoulder. Then he took another squint out of the window, put out his left arm and levelled the pistol, waited until the coach was relatively stable for a second and the weaving figure of one of their pursuers was in line with his sight, then he pulled the trigger, and was rewarded by a scream from his target and a cheer from the roof.

"Got im!" shouted Mr. Petts. "'E's fell orf 'is 'orse!"

"Well done, sir!" cried Jem, loosing off another barrel. "Ar, bloody 'ell! Missed 'im agen!"

"Try aiming," Sir Richard advised.

"Can't keep 'im on the sight long enough, wot with the drag jouncing and 'im crahched on 'is mount's neck. I can't get a decent pull at 'im. Ar, bloody 'ell!"

The repetition of the expletive was due to a shot from the remaining pursuer, which struck the barrel of Jem's gun and almost knocked it out of his hands.

"I'll allow your language has some justification in the stress of the moment," Sir Richard remarked judicially, "but you don't need to repeat yourself! You do have quite an extensive repertoire!"

"'E ain't arf dented your good shotgun!" Jem said indignantly, inspecting the damage.

Sir Richard leaned across and took the weapon from him, while Jem picked up its partner and peered out of the window.

"Now that is excessively provoking!" Sir Richard said, looking at the ugly mark on the gun-barrel. "Joe won't be at all pleased about that!" He cocked the one still-loaded barrel preparatory to firing it and leaned forward to manoeuvre it out of the window.

At that moment, the coach struck a particularly vicious pothole and gave such a violent lurch that Sir Richard was thrown forward and landed heavily on top of Miss Minster, knocking or twisting his knee in some way as he did so. Miss Minster thought he had been shot, for he gave a cry of pain and well-nigh fainted.

"Richard! Where are you hurt?" she exclaimed, struggling to free herself from his weight and move him into a position where she could attend to his wound. A blinding flash of self-knowledge suddenly made her understand only too clearly why she was so cast-down at the thought of parting from him.

"Damned knee!" he said through clenched teeth, shaking his head in an effort to clear it. "Where the devil is that gun? It's cocked and will go off at a touch!"

"On the seat," Mr. Tupper replied nervously. "Shall I . . . ?"

Sir Richard raised his head and saw that the shotgun had landed safely on the seat where Miss Minster had been sitting earlier. "No, leave it. It's safe enough there. Oh God! My knee!" He laid his head on Miss Minster's shoulder and closed his eyes. She held him and stroked his hair, not knowing quite what else to do, filled with a tender longing to ease his pain.

"You're not shot, then?" she asked.

He stirred and settled his head more comfortably. "No. I jarred m'knee, that's all. I'll be recovered in a minute."

Jem, his attention divided between his master, his own need to hold on to the strap to keep his place, and his desire to get in another shot at their pursuer, admonished Miss Minster not to try to lift Sir Richard.

"'E's too 'eavy for yer! Let 'im bide where 'e is for a bit—'e'll come to no 'arm there, and I'll come and give 'im a 'and when things is settled dahn!"

Nevertheless, Miss Minster contrived to give Sir Richard a little more room and helped him to sit up and straighten his leg.

"That's easier," he said, wincing. "I'm sorry I descended on you like that. Did I hurt you?"

"No."

"I thought you cried out."

"I believed you to be wounded."

He raised his head and looked at her curiously for a moment, and then was distracted by an urgent need to hold on as the coach was progressing in a series of wild leaps and bounds, jolting as if it would disintegrate. There were sounds of alarm from the roof, accompanied by a slithering sound. The inside passengers looked up, and Mr. Tupper exclaimed, "Oh, pray God no-one has fallen off!"

Jem stuck his head out of the window and shouted "What's to do?" pulling it in again quickly as a bullet narrowly missed him.

"Black nearly fell orf!" Mr. Petts shouted back. "''Is darbies saved 'im. You all right down there?"

"Merry as grigs!" Jem replied, hanging on with both hands as the coach appeared to be about to leave the road altogether.

There was another tremendous roar from the guard's blunderbuss, followed by a wild shriek of "Got 'im!" from that worthy.

"Well done!" said Sir Richard.

"Sir says yer done well!" Jem shouted from the window. "Nah can we slow dahn?"

"'Orses are bolting!" Mr. Petts replied cheerfully. "'Ang on—dragsman's doing 'is best!"

"Who said 'evil news rides post'?" Sir Richard murmured, returning his head to Miss Minster's shoulder.

"Milton," she replied. "In *Samson Agonistes*." Her voice was remarkably steady, under the circumstances, and only her painfully tight grip on Sir Richard's arm betrayed her fear.

The motion of the coach appeared to grow worse, and it became necessary for him to put both arms round her very tightly and brace himself against the seat to prevent them being thrown about, and then, quite suddenly, they began to slow down.

"'Ell, 'Ull and 'Alifax!" said Jem. "Nah I knows why they calls a stage-coach a 'God-permit'! 'Ow the 'ell 'as 'e managed to slow them?"

"We're going uphill," Mr. Tupper replied shakily. "And kindly watch your language!" at which Jem apologised handsomely.

As the hill grew steeper, the horses slowed to a canter, then to a walk, and then the coachman could be heard crying "Whoa, there!" and they stopped.

In a trice, the guard was down and had the nearside door open, anxiously enquiring after the welfare of his passengers, who assured him they were very well, all things considered. Mr. Tupper was soon hauled up on his seat, and then the guard and Jem set about getting Sir Richard up. Once he was deposited in his place, looking distinctly done-up, Mr. Kirby, who had been hovering in the background, darted forward and assisted Miss Minster to descend to the road, and stood gazing at her with a mixture of anxiety and admiration, pouring out exclamations of horror that she should have been subjected to such an ordeal, and praise for her calmness and courage, while she brushed the straw from her skirts and wished he would be quiet and leave her alone.

"I shall just walk up and down for a few minutes," she said when he eventually ran down. "If you will excuse me."

"I—I have been seeking an opportunity to have a word with you alone," he said tentatively. "Perhaps . . . ?"

"Later, if you will be so kind," she replied abstractedly. "I must have a moment to myself to recover—you understand," and she walked away from him to the other side of the road, where she stood looking along the valley below and the ridge on which they were halted, towards what looked like a circle of standing stones, hardly aware of what he had just said, her thoughts filled with the ridiculous, hopeless knowledge that she was in love with Richard Severall.

Mr. Kirby tactfully returned to the coach to enquire after Sir Richard and to assist Jem in drawing the remaining charges from the guns and packing them away.

After a while, the coachman declared himself satisfied with the state of his cattle, and the passengers reembarked, the guard going over to rouse Miss Minster from her reverie, anxiously enquiring if she felt quite well.

"Yes, thank you," she replied, and managed a smile as he handed her to her place.

Sir Richard had recovered by now, and appeared much as usual, apart from being a little pale. He replied to her enquiry with, "Pretty tolerable, thank you. It hurts when I jar or twist it, but soon dies down. I'm sorry I frightened you."

She managed a wan smile in return, and stared out of the window as the coach moved off.

In another quarter of an hour or so, they slowed for the guard to put on the drag-shoe, and then turned left-handed down a steep hill, the wheelers leaning back hard to hold the coach and the drag squealing horribly, like a massacre of pigs. Half-way down they came upon the first houses of Keswick, and, after another slowing at the bottom for the drag to be taken off again, trotted smartly past the church to the Market Square, where they drew up outside the new Moot Hall, finished, as Mr. Tupper proudly informed them, only a few weeks before.

The guard and Mr. Petts got down and consulted with Mr. Tupper about the whereabouts of the office of the Commissioner for Oaths. It was decided that the coach would leave Mr. Petts and his prisoner here, and go on to the office, where the Bow Street Runner would join them as soon as may be, having deposited Black in the lock-up, and the coach would go to the inn and await them there.

Mr. Petts climbed up again and unshackled his prisoner from the roof-rail, and then helped him down, his wrists still being manacled. Sir Richard suddenly opened the door and got down, leaning very heavily on his stick, and went to intercept them in the arches of the Moot Hall.

"Just a minute!" he said. "I—er—I wouldn't wish you to feel I bear any grudge against you." This was to Black. "In fact, I wonder if I can help you in any way?"

Black gave him a puzzled look and replied, "Your 'eart's as soft as your 'ead! What could you do for a man in my sityation?"

"I could hire you a good lawyer. He might be able to save your life."

Black stared at him for a moment, and then said, "Well, you're a gentry-cove, I 'as to admit! I'd rather take a quick end with 'empen fever on Newman's lift than a

slow 'un inside 'is 'otel with gaol fever, or in Van Die-
man's Land. Never could abide the sea.''

Sir Richard delved inside his voluminous redingote and
produced one of his cards, which he put in Black's pocket.
''If you change your mind, there's my address.''

''Thankee,'' Black, replied a trifle curtly, but he gave
Sir Richard's proffered hand a brief shake before turning
to trudge inside the Moot Hall with his captor. Sir Richard watched him go, and then returned to the coach,
which drove off towards the Commissioner's office.

''I'm glad you did that,'' Miss Minster said softly.
''One cannot help but feel sorry for him.''

They arrived at the office of Mr. Tupper's acquaintance in a few minutes, for Keswick was a small town. The
office was in the Commissioner's house, a pleasant mod-
ern double-fronted building with a white stuccoed front,
which opened straight from the street. A ring at the bell
by the black front door in its neat porch brought an elderly clerk to let them in. He recognised Mr. Tupper and
ushered him and his companions in to a small sitting-
room on the right of the square hall, and invited them to
be seated while he fetched his master.

Miss Minster sat down on a small sofa and looked
around the rather dark and shabby room, which was lined
with glass-fronted bookcases full of musty-looking books,
and thought how pleasant it could have been made with a
little bright chintz, some flowers, and a more generous fire
than the three fragments of coal which burned grudgingly in the too-small fireplace. Mr. Kirby stationed himself behind her in a protective manner, and Sir Richard
limped across and sat opposite her in a heavy, clumsy-
looking chair, rather distantly related in design to the
works of Mr. Chippendale—a remote trans-Pennine
fourteenth cousin, perhaps. Jem stood stolidly by the

door, his little bright eyes darting about and taking in every detail of the room, and Mr. Tupper peered hopefully into one of the bookcases as if seeking some rare treasure of legal case-history.

Presently, the door opened, and they were joined by a tall, thin austere-looking man in very plain, dark clothes. He wore gold-rimmed spectacles and stared severely at his visitors through them as he offered three fingers to Mr. Tupper, who made his companions and Mr. Carron known to each other, and explained the reason for their visit.

Mr. Carron rapidly arranged for a bevy of clerks to take statements from them, each in a different room, as they must not give their evidence in one another's presence. Ascertaining that Jem had nothing to impart of any consequence, Mr. Carron dismissed him with a lordly, "You may wait in the hall," at which Jem nodded gravely, and the moment Mr. Carron's back was turned, stuck out his tongue and crossed his eyes in a delightfully hideous grimace which quite lifted Miss Minster's spirits.

The gentlemen went out with their respective clerks, and Mr. Carron returned in a few minutes with a sheaf of paper, a handful of pens and an ink-stand, sat down at a small table near Miss Minster, and intimated that he intended to do her the courtesy of taking down her statement himself. At his invitation, she moved to a chair at the same table.

First of all, he urged her to tell him in her own words what had occurred. She began with a brief account of the actors involved, and how they came to be at the Nag's Head, and then plunged into a description of the events in the dining-parlour from the moment Black got up and went to the window. Mr. Carron listened carefully, interrupting with a question from time to time, until she reached the point when Mr. Petts snapped the handcuffs and arrested the highwayman.

He stopped her there, gave her a stiff and frosty smile, and informed her that she made an admirable witness. Then he asked her to tell him the whole story again, slowly, while he wrote it down.

Almost at the end of this second telling, she suddenly found tears running down her cheeks. She apologised to Mr. Carron and tried to stop them, wiping angrily at her eyes with her handkerchief and trying to go on with her account, but Mr. Carron said that he could manage the rest from her first telling. He went to the door and spoke to someone outside in the hall.

Returning to the table, he continued to write, and for a while there was silence, apart from the scratching of his pen and an occasional snap from the fire. Miss Minster managed to stop crying by the exercise of a considerable amount of will-power, and then there was a tap at the door, and a maid came in with a small tray bearing a cup of tea, a cream-jug and a sugar-basin, which she put at Miss Minster's elbow. The cup contained a pretty strong brew, which she drank gratefully, after stirring in a spoonful of cream.

Mr. Carron finished writing, having covered two or three sheets of foolscap, then sanded the last page, shook it clear, and scanned the whole thing through from the beginning.

"Yes, that seems... Now, madam, please read this, and tell me if it is incorrect, even in the smallest detail."

Miss Minster read the pages slowly and carefully, aware that a man's life would depend on what she had said, finding one or two small errors, which Mr. Carron corrected, asking her to initial each one. The wording was not at all her own, being very formal and speckled with "aforesaids" and "hereins", but it set out the story very precisely and clearly, and when she had read it all, she handed it back to Mr. Carron with a firm "Yes, that's quite correct."

"Now it must be copied," he said. "I'll not keep you long," and hurried from the room, calling for someone named Simon as he went.

Miss Minster sat by the table, idly running one finger to and fro along the grain of the wood, trying not to think about the day's events. The only alternative seemed to be her own future, and she found little comfort in wondering yet again about the Partridge family.

Presently, she thought a little further ahead, and wondered if Sir Richard would actually carry out his declared intention of bringing his sister to visit her, and if Sir Marmaduke would allow her to receive such a visit. The faint little hope that she might see Sir Richard again seemed like a very, very fine thread of gold in the dark fabric of the future.

"What shall I do if I never see him again?" she thought. "How can I bear it?" and the tears ran down her cheeks again, taking all her will-power to make them stop.

Soon after, Mr. Carron returned with her statement and a copy, bringing a clerk with him. He requested Miss Minster to read through her statement again aloud, while the clerk checked the copy against it. She was then asked to sign the original at the foot of each page, and on the final page, where he and the clerk added their own signatures as witnesses. Then Mr. Carron wrote some more below the signatures, and requested Miss Minster to swear an oath to the truth of her statement, the clerk producing a Testament for the purpose.

After some more signing and witnessing, Mr. Carron folded the copy of the statement and gave it to her, telling her to keep it safely, so that she would know what she had said if there was any question about it later, and warned her that she might still be required to attend the trial, if it was necessary to question her about anything in her evidence. He took the signed statement to give to Mr. Petts, when he should arrive.

As that was apparently all, she was then left alone to await the return of the others, and in a few minutes, Mr. Kirby came hurrying in and exclaimed dramatically, "Ah, at last I find you alone!"

"Did you wish to say something to me," she asked, vaguely recalling that he had said something of the sort earlier.

"Indeed, yes!" He went to stand by the fireplace and gave her a sidelong, nervous look, running an agitated hand over his golden curls. "The fact is, my dear lady—I have taken a great liking to you—a very great liking indeed . . ." He hesitated, and finding that she was regarding him with a puzzled look in her wide grey eyes, was apparently encouraged to go on, speaking in a fast and nervous manner. "This being so, and I flatter myself you are not—er—insensible to my—er—better aspects—I—er—that is, I would like to make you a—er—proposal."

"A proposal!" she exclaimed, horrified.

"Indeed, and one I think you will find—well—not unattractive. I trust you find Keswick quite a pleasant little town?"

"Yes, it does seem attractive, but Mr. Kirby . . ."

"Now, I happen to own a little house in Keswick," he went on, blithely ignoring her attempted protest. "It's not unlike this one," with a comprehensive gesture indicating their surroundings. "It is standing empty at present, and I should be very happy to make that house over to you, for your very own, to stand in your name." He paused, as if expecting a reply, but Miss Minster was struck dumb with shock, so he continued, "And furnished, of course, to your taste. There would be an allowance, paid quarterly, and I think you will find it quite a generous sum, for I assure you I'm not at all a mean man where my pleasures are concerned, and you will also find me liberal in the matter of dresses and—er—trinkets! You will be able to live in becoming style, as befits a lady of your distinction and personal attractions, and I shall be able to visit you quite frequently—say three or four times a week, with perfect discretion and—er—convenience."

He seemed to have warmed to his task now he was fully launched into his speech, and was smiling upon Miss Minster with all the charm and confidence to be expected of a very handsome young man of considerable fortune, fully aware of his attraction for the fair sex in both respects, and it did not seem to occur to him that the present recipient of his smile was not showing any sign of swooning with delight at his generous offer.

"And, to be very business-like and forward-looking," he continued happily, "when the times comes, as come, alas, it eventually must, although not, I sincerely hope, until very far in the future—when, I say"—keeping very good control over this sentence, which had already convoluted its way through five parentheses—"the time comes for us to part at last, there will, of course, be a parting gift of such generous proportions as, I am sure, will leave you fully contented!" He came to a halt and stood awaiting her answer, his fine blue eyes alight with enthusiasm and expectation.

"Are you, by any chance, inviting me to become your mistress?" Miss Minster enquired in a level and exceedingly calm voice.

"Oh. Well. If you wish to put it so bluntly," he replied, clearly disconcerted. "In a word, yes!"

"I have never been so insulted in all my life!" Miss Minster said coldly. "Kindly remove yourself and your insolent offer at once!"

Mr. Kirby's confident smile vanished and was replaced by an expression of incredulous shock. "But—but I thought..." he stammered.

"Then you thought wrongly!"

"You—you surely didn't expect an offer of *marriage*?" he said, more coherently, but still very much taken aback. "I mean—you haven't anything much to offer in the marriage-stakes, have you?"

"Please go away!" Miss Minster said, her voice shaking a little. "I neither wished nor expected *anything* from you!"

"Well, as you please." To Mr. Kirby's credit, he did not lose his temper, but walked to the door with dignity. He paused with his hand on the knob and said quite reasonably, "You may feel indignant about it now, but no doubt you'll feel differently when you've had time to consider the matter. It would be interesting to see precisely how much your precious virtue is worth when it comes to repaying Severall the money he has lent you! I'll warrant that by the time he's finished with you, and you've found out what the Partridges are like, you'll be glad to come running back to me! You'll find me at Kirby Hall, on the Penrith road, and the offer will still be open."

Miss Minster had risen to her feet and turned her back on him, and was apparently looking out of the window. She made no reply, and in fact only half-heard what he said as she was trying very hard not to burst into tears of mingled shock at receiving such an offer, and misery that it should be the wrong man who wanted her, even on those terms.

Mr. Kirby went out and carefully refrained from slamming the door behind him. He encountered Sir Richard, Mr. Tupper and Mr. Petts in the hall, and bade them farewell in a courteous, if rather preoccupied manner, which Sir Richard noted with interest, and then departed for his home without more ado.

Mr. Petts collected his affidavits from Mr. Carron, and was just saying his own farewells when Miss Minster emerged, pale but composed, from the sitting-room, in time to shake hands with him and receive her slightly sardonic wish for a pleasant end to the journey, and then she left with the others to seek the coach.

The guard was waiting outside when they arrived at the inn on Main Street, looking anxiously for them as the afternoon was now well advanced. He agreed that fifteen minutes either way would make little difference, and admitted that the horses were not yet harnessed, although that would take only a few minutes, when Sir Richard insisted that they should take tea before setting off.

Miss Minster thought apprehensively of her dwindling resources and the prospect of arriving in Cockermouth too late to reach the Partridges' house that night, but Sir Richard dismissed her attempt to express her fears with a brisk "Don't worry about all that! I'll see to it for you," and when she pointed out that she was already far advanced in debt to him, he simply repeated "We'll sort all that out later. Come and drink your tea."

CHAPTER ELEVEN

THE TEA HAD TO BE DRUNK standing, and scalding hot, with the guard fidgetting in the doorway, and it was, in fact, less than fifteen minutes before he had his remaining four passengers herded back to their conveyance, which they found had now six horses harnessed to it.

"How far is Cockermouth from here?" Miss Minster asked the guard as he handed her to her place.

"Two stages. About fifteen miles, madam," he replied. "They're short stages, for t'first is ower t'Whinlatter, which is very steep in places."

Sir Richard enquired what had become of their original driver, and was informed that he lived in Keswick and had been literally carried off by his anxious family, at which Sir Richard requested the guard to convey a small gift to him at the first opportunity, handing over some coin, which the guard carefully wrapped in a piece of paper, making a note on its amount, source and destination on the outside before stowing it away in one of his inmost pockets.

The relief coachman was being very particular about his tackle, carefully tugging and peering at traces, belly bands, breechings and bridles. When he was satisfied, he lit the lamps on the coach, for it was already dusk, and then climbed on the box. Jem, who had been standing with his head out of the window watching, sat down and cheered his fellow-passengers with the information that he had heard of the case of a dragsman finding the ribbon of his nearside leader jammed when he tried to take a left-hand corner a little too fast, and had run slap into a waggon coming the opposite way, breaking his own neck, killing his off-side cattle, and injuring most of his passengers.

"Thank you for that edifying information," Sir Richard said mildly. "Now I suggest you put a lock on your gans until you have something more encouraging to say!"

"Sir!" replied Jem, and then obediently shut his mouth.

The coach shot away with the team already reaching a trot as they swung into Main Street and clattered over the stones, the guard sounding his horn as a warning to clear the way for His Majesty's Mail—although he was not actually carrying any on this run. Miss Minster caught a glimpse of Mr. Petts under a lamp in the street, the ear-flaps of his moleskin cap untied and flopping a little, giving him the look of a melancholy beagle. She waved, and he lifted a hand in salute as the coach swept past.

Mr. Tupper kindly, if belatedly, reminded them that Mr. Southey, the new Poet Laureate, lived in Keswick, with the family of Mr. Coleridge, who had abandoned them some years before. He obviously considered this a very peculiar circumstance, and said he could not understand why the Wordsworths remained on friendly terms with such an irresponsible person.

"I suppose they feel that there is some right on his side," Miss Minster observed charitably, assuming correctly that Mr. Tupper was referring to Mr. Coleridge, not the worthy and estimable Mr. Southey.

"I feel there can be no excuse for leaving a wife and young children to starve while he gallyvants abroad!" Mr.

Tupper exclaimed. "Besides, they say," his voice sinking to a shocked whisper, "that he eats opium!"

"Many poets do," Sir Richard pointed out. "Damned silly habit, in my opinion, but they claim it enhances their awareness of their surroundings, and so improves their poetry. It ruins their health as well, of course."

"Indeed!" Mr. Tupper replied. "The Wordsworths have let their old cottage to a Mr. de Quincey, who also has this pernicious habit, and they say he keeps laudanum in a decanter, and drinks it as another might take sherry wine!" He shook his head and brooded over the matter for a while.

Miss Minster felt a great depression of spirits creeping over her at the thought of the imminent parting from Sir Richard, which came nearer with every creak and rumble of the coach, and tried to distract herself by looking out of the window, but she could make out very little in the growing darkness, although Mr. Tupper roused himself from his thoughts after a while and said that they were now passing the head of Derwentwater, and might catch a glimpse of Bassenthwaite Lake on their right. In fact, as the road began to climb near Braithwaite, a stretch of water could be seen glimmering away in the distance, with the great white heights of Blencathra and Skiddaw rising behind. They looked exceedingly cold and grim, and when Mr. Tupper named them and said that, had there been more light, they might have caught a fleeting glimpse of Scafell Pike itself away to the south beyond Derwentwater, she was filled with a firm conviction that she did not wish to see it, or any other mountain, but wanted to return at once to the low hills and pleasant green country in the south.

Beyond Braithwaite, the road began to climb steeply in a diagonal fashion across the great mass of a huge fell which seemed to rise vertically to the sky, and Jem exclaimed, "'Ere, we ain't going over the top of that thing, I 'ope?" in tones of alarm.

"No, no!" Mr. Tupper replied soothingly. "That is Grisedale Pike. The road slips round the corner and passes between it and Lorton Fells."

Jem expressed relief. In a few minutes, the coach stopped, and the guard appeared at the door to request him and Mr. Tupper to walk the next section, which was particularly steep, and had become icy as they were so late, so that even a six-team could not manage the laden coach. Mr. Tupper sighed, but Jem got out with alacrity and asked if he might help lead the horses up the incline, an offer which the guard gracefully accepted.

The coach started off again, going very slowly, the horses leaning into their collars and trying their foothold at every step, Jem urging them on with strange incantations and occasional bursts of song, which they seemed to find encouraging. Miss Minster and Sir Richard moved to the middle of the coach, and he tried to see something of her face in the dim light of the little oil lamps above their heads.

"I assume you refused George Kirby, then?" he asked diffidently, after a lengthy silence.

"Yes, of course. Did you know he meant to make me an offer, then? If so, it would have been a kindness to warn me, for it came as something of a shock!"

"Well, I only suspected he might have it in mind. He was obviously very taken with you. He didn't tell me his intentions, however. I thought female intuition always warned young ladies of impending proposals?"

"I had no idea—it was extremely embarrassing."

"Oh, I'm sorry—I thought you liked him very well." Sir Richard sounded puzzled.

"I did. I thought him a very pleasant young man, but it didn't enter my head that he had any thought of such a thing! It was mortifying to find he thought me fallen so low as to consider accepting such an offer!"

Apparently light suddenly dawned on Sir Richard, for he exclaimed in the tones of one making an important discovery, "Didn't he offer you marriage, then?"

"No, he did not!"

"What, then?"

Miss Minster hesitated, but her hurt feelings and growing unhappiness banished discretion, and she said in a voice of quiet despair, "An establishment in Keswick, with a quarterly allowance and the promise of a parting honorarium when he grew tired of me!"

"Damned insolence!" Sir Richard exclaimed. "I've a good mind to go over to Keswick tomorrow and give the puppy a piece of my mind. I wonder where I could borrow a horsewhip!"

"Oh, please don't!" Miss Minster exclaimed in alarm. "I can't afford such a scandal!"

"No, I suppose it would be unpleasant," Sir Richard sounded regretful. "I'm sorry—I really thought he meant to ask you to marry him."

"It doesn't matter." Miss Minster tried to blink back the tears which were filling her eyes, and groped in her reticule for her already damp handkerchief. One drop fell on the rug, which Sir Richard had given her as soon as they started out, and glistened in the dim light. Sir Richard silently handed her a handkerchief of his own, very large and white, still crisply folded from its laundering, which she received with a doleful little word of thanks, and blotted her cheeks with it.

"Did you like him so very much?" he asked quietly.

"No. He seemed a pleasant sort of young man—a little conceited and given to gushing, but I'd no idea he had any particular interest in me, except to flirt with me a little, to pass the time."

"You're not heart-broken, then?"

"No. Not over Mr. Kirby!" she replied with careful accuracy. "Just mortified and insulted, 'though, as he said, I could hardly expect anything more, not having anything to offer myself!"

Sir Richard considered what she had said for a few minutes in silence, while she dried her tears and tried to pull herself together.

"You won't be able to go beyond Cockermouth tonight, you know," he said at length.

"I don't know what I shall do," she replied. "I hope the Partridges will have sent a conveyance for me, but they may not know that the relief coach was sent, and in that case, they will probably not be expecting me today. I hope there will be a message for me, at least, when we arrive at the inn."

"You've had a singularly trying day. I think you should stay overnight in Cockermouth and face the future in the morning, when you're rested and refreshed. I shall certainly not attempt to go any further tonight."

"I cannot afford it," she said flatly.

"I do wish you would stop worrying about that! We'll have dinner when we get to the inn, and talk for a while, and then you shall have an early night. I'll invite Tupper to dine with us, so you'll have a chaperon, and I promise that before you retire, we'll have all your financial problems worked out in a satisfactory manner. And I'll not hear a word of protest!" he added severely, as she seemed about to utter several such words. "You ain't that eager to get to the Partridges', are you?"

"I don't want to go at all!" she blurted out. "I hate this country! It's so bleak and harsh! I want to go home!" and she sobbed bitterly.

Sir Richard, knowing she had no home to go to, was silent, but he moved over to her side of the coach and put a comforting arm round her shoulders so that she could cry into the folds of his redingote until she felt better.

After a while, she raised her head and resolutely wiped her eyes, and said, "Thank you. I'm sorry to make such a fuss."

"Not at all," he replied. "I was just wondering..."

But what he was about to say had to remain unsaid for the time being, as the coach had stopped at the top of the steep rise, and Mr. Tupper and Jem were about to climb in again. Sir Richard returned to his corner and Miss Minster to hers, and she sat staring into the outer darkness, while he appeared to be listening with interest to Mr. Tupper discoursing to Jem on the theories of Mr. Hutton and Mr. Playfair of the Royal Society of Edinburgh concerning the influence of wind, weather, ice and running water in the formation of all these mountains, lakes and valleys, which, as Jem said, "Fair mikes yer fink!"

The road ran straight and slightly downhill for a time, and then they stopped again for the drag-shoe to go on, and Miss Minster became aware of the scene at which she was staring. It was a snowy waste, rising sheer from the roadside, dotted with lumps of rock, bathed in moonlight, and looking as eerie and harsh as the landscape of a nightmare.

"It ain't a prepossessing sight," Sir Richard remarked dispassionately. "Fine enough in a painting, no doubt, provided it hangs in a comfortable room with a good fire roaring up the chimney!"

"Whinlatter Pass is considered a very fine and impressive piece of scenery!" Mr. Tupper sounded a trifle offended.

"Oh, so it is!" Sir Richard assured him. "But not exactly comforting on a winter's night!"

The coach crawled slowly down a steep hill with a particularly nasty double bend, the drag screeching banshee-like on the turns. Jem put his head out of the window and observed, "'Strewth! It looks like the Gawdyramas out 'ere! I never knew we 'ad mahntins like this in England! I fort 'Ighgate 'Ill was 'igh fer us!"

"Scafell Pike," Mr. Tupper informed him, "is the seventh highest mountain in Europe, and is higher than anything you may have seen in Spain!"

"Garn?" Jem said, shutting the window. "And 'ere 'ave I been gawping at all them mahntins in Spine, when I could 'ave come 'ere and seen better, wivout the trouble of getting shot at by Johnny Crapoh!"

"Only the trouble of being shot at by your own countrymen!" Sir Richard pointed out. "I wasn't aware that you went to Spain to look at mountains, Jem!"

"You 'as to look at 'em when you're chasing Johnnies all over 'em!" Jem replied. "I prefers it flattish meself."

"Good arable and a neat piece of coppice," Miss Minster quoted softly, with such a wealth of feeling in her voice that Sir Richard suddenly stared at her very intently, but her face was turned away from the faint light into the shadows.

Once they had descended the pass and changed horses at High Lorton, where the guard rather grudgingly allowed them ten minutes for a warming drink, there was only a very straightforward run of less than an hour to Cockermouth, and this was accomplished at a steady trot. On the way, Sir Richard invited Mr. Tupper to dine on arrival, and the solicitor accepted with thanks, as he said that his housekeeper would probably not be expecting him, and would have no meal prepared.

"My wife passed on some years ago," he confided, "and both my sons are married and moved away, one to Carlisle and the other to Appleby. I expect my housekeeper will have been worried, but she would have enough sense to enquire of the postmaster what has happened to us."

"M'sister will have done the same," Sir Richard said, "'though she'll have been more miffed than worried. She's always convinced that any mishap befalling me is entirely due to m'careless nature. She says I'm an irresponsible idiot, which I ain't in the least!"

"Indeed not!" Mr. Tupper exclaimed. "I must say I have never detected the slightest element of irresponsibility or carelessness in your nature! I would really not advise your lady sister to maintain such calumnies against you! So misleading, and probably damaging to your reputation!"

He was possibly about to go on to advise Sir Richard to sue his sister for slander, but at this point they arrived in Cockermouth, and he turned his attention to the business of getting off the coach and retrieving his baggage instead.

At a word from Sir Richard, Jem hurried into the inn, leaving his master to supervise the unloading of their baggage and tip the guard and driver. He directed the hall porter to take in Miss Minster's small trunk as well, but did not demur when she chose to give her vails herself. She had handed the guard a whole crown, feeling that he deserved it, and a half-crown to the driver, which left her with only a few coppers, as far as she knew.

Jem was in the hall when they went in, and he informed them that he had bespoken a private dining-parlour and two front bedrooms for them, and that dinner would be ready in half an hour. Miss Minster looked about for her trunk, but it had already been taken upstairs, and when she then said that she must enquire if there was a message for her, Jem said there was, and proffered a folded and sealed sheet of paper, but his master intercepted it and said firmly, "You shall have it later, when you've eaten and rested," then took her by the elbow and propelled her firmly towards the stairs, telling her to go up and inspect her room and get herself ready for dinner.

"But..." she began.

"I can't stand a female who keeps butting!" Sir Richard said severely. "Worse than goats!" and shooed her up the stairs, following himself at his slower pace.

A chambermaid conducted Miss Minster to her room on the first floor, and she found it to be one of the best—and most expensive—neatly furnished, with a large tester bed, and a fire burning in the hearth. A can of hot water and her trunk were all ready for her. She removed her outdoor clothing and her dress and hung them up, and then washed and put on a fresh dress from her trunk, which was only a little creased.

As she was combing her hair and trying to make a rough estimate of how much she now owed Sir Richard, and worrying about how she would repay him if it came to more than the ten pounds she would receive in June, she suddenly recalled Mr. Kirby's parting speech from the door of Mr. Carron's sitting-room, or, at least, one sentence of it, which seemed to have registered in her memory, if not in her consciousness at the time it was uttered. "It will be interesting to see precisely how much your

precious virtue is worth when it come to repaying Severall the money he has lent you!''

She sat quite still, staring at her reflection in the mirror
as a number of factors came together in her shocked
mind—Mr. Kirby's words, Sir Richard's repeated refusal
to discuss the matter, always deferring it until later, his
insistence that she should stay the night here, the uncon-
sciously-noted fact that he had gone into the room next
door when he came upstairs. It was all too obvious to her
now, and she could not think why she had failed to realise it before! Of course, that was how he intended to receive repayment of his loan—in kind, or, rather, in
''kindness''!

Presumably, they would pass the evening together, and
retire when Mr. Tupper left, and then, after a suitable interval, there would be a discreet tap at her door, and a
murmured suggestion . . . and she could not refuse him!

She realised that very clearly indeed. Quite apart from
the problem of finding any other way of paying her debt
if he said he would not wait until June, she could not refuse him because she had been fool enough to fall in love
with him! Somehow, the moral aspects of the matter
seemed remarkably unimportant against her longing for
him, and she found herself thinking quite philosophi-
cally that at least it would be one very wonderful night to
remember for the rest of her lonely, wretched life!

The sound of uneven footsteps and the tap of a stick
passing her door roused her from her thoughts, and she
hastily finished arranging her hair and went out of the
room to follow Sir Richard downstairs. Jem was just
coming out of the next room, and he looked at her for a
second, and then asked in a hoarse, conspiratorial voice
if he might have a word with her.

"Of course. What is it?"

"It's abaht the Colonel. 'E's a good man, you knows, and very kind. Always 'elps anybody 'e can."

"Yes, I know."

"'E don't orfen ask anyfink for 'isself."

Miss Minster's heart gave a little lurch, for this sounded a complete confirmation of her recent thoughts, but she had not expected Sir Richard to leave his servant to make the arrangements for her seduction.

"So, if 'e was to ask you somefink, and you was to feel you could siy yes to 'im, 'e wouldn't never give you no cause ter be sorry for it arterwards."

There was silence for a few seconds as she waited for the next move, and then Jem said awkwardly, "I'm speaking aht er turn agen. Sorry. Didn't mean no 'arm. Wouldn't wanter see 'im un'appy fer want o' somebody ter siy a word for 'im, like. You won't tell 'im I said anyfink?"

"No. I shall not tell him. I respect your loyalty and affection for him," she replied truthfully, for Jem's good intentions were patently obvious.

He gave her a little bobbing bow, and she went on down the stairs, feeling very confused and anxious, not sure whether to believe that Jem had spoken without his master's knowledge or not.

A porter directed her to the private room which Sir Richard had taken, and she found him there in earnest conversation with Mr. Tupper, but he broke off as she entered and invited her to take her place at the table, which was a small, round one, set for three. He gave a hearty tug at the bell-pull by the hearth before taking his own seat. Mr. Tupper was already in his place.

There was a short wait, during which Miss Minster looked about the room, which was panelled in dark wood, with dark oak furniture, and had a sombre appearance, only lightened by a cheerful blaze in the hearth and the clean white cloth on the table. Heavy brown stuff curtains covered the window, and an elaborately carved Coromandel chest stood on the floor under it, where Mr. Tupper had deposited his hat, greatcoat and valise.

Sir Richard enquired if her room was satisfactory, and she had hardly replied when the first course of the meal made its entrance—a tureen of mutton broth, served by a maid. It appeared that Sir Richard had already ordered, as the rest followed without any instructions being given. There were potted shrimps served with toast, which Mr. Tupper said were a local delicacy, dabs rolled in breadcrumbs and fried, roast beef, a rabbit pie, and vegetables.

"Ain't the beef to your fancy?" Sir Richard asked Miss Minster suddenly, in an interval in Mr. Tupper's flow of conversation, thereby proving himself less unaware of her abstraction than he appeared. "It's a mite tough, I believe. Take a little of the pie instead."

Miss Minster thanked him, but said that the beef was quite good. "I'm just not very hungry," she admitted.

"Try a little," he repeated coaxingly. "You must keep up your strength, for you have to face a fearful ordeal tonight!"

Miss Minster stared at him, her eyes wide with shock, her mind immediately forming a link between this extraordinary statement and her suspicions about his intentions.

He gave her a puzzled look and explained, "Jem is to make his debut as an actor, and I could not help but promise we should attend the performance to lend him support. The mummers are to play here tonight, and one of their number is sick, so Jem has offered to take his place."

"What—what role is he to play?" Miss Minster stammered in relief at finding his meaning not so cruelly blatant as she had feared.

"The front legs of St. George's horse, I understand," Sir Richard replied, cunningly placing a large slice of rabbit pie on her plate while her attention was distracted.

"And has he any experience of playing such a part?" she enquired.

"None whatever, but he knows a deal about horses. They usually bite him if they get the chance, so perhaps he means to take his revenge. I can't think why they do, anyway, for he's a very considerate rider. Perhaps they like his flavour!"

Miss Minster could not help but smile, which lifted her spirits a little, and she was able to make a better showing at eating her dinner, managing the pie, and a moderate helping of plum duff, which was not quite as light as it might have been. She took a little burgundy with the meat, and was persuaded to a half-glass of madeira with the cheese. She had not tasted it before, and found it pleasant.

After dinner, a waiter summoned them to the play, and they decided to leave tea until afterwards. They adjourned to the main public room of the inn, where they found some thirty or so people already assembled, seated on benches round three sides of the room, leaving a fair-sized arena for the mummers. The innkeeper took them to three chairs in the centre of the front row, from which he ejected three persons of lesser importance. Sir Richard protested at this, but the displaced spectators assured him that they had no objections, having seen the play many times before, and went off happily to consume ale at Sir Richard's expense.

Presently, the mummers filed in from another room, where they had put on their costumes. There was a herald, dressed in a sack-cloth tabard painted with a rather improbable coat-of-arms, a doctor in an elderly suit which must once have belonged to a gentleman, but had come down in the world during the last thirty years or so. It had been made for someone with a much greater girth than the present wearer. This was crowned by a moth-eaten bag-wig and a demi-bateau with its brim turned down all round.

St. George wore cord breeches, worsted stockings and wooden-soled boots, and a very white, beautifully embroidered smock, and carried a large wooden sword and a shield painted with his red cross. The glory of his costume was a real mediaeval tilting-helmet with a barred visor, open at present so that he could see and be heard, and topped with a plume of decidedly tatty ostrich feathers. He was accompanied by his horse, a beast of obvious mettle and intelligence, coloured rather curiously, as his coat appeared to be made of old sacks and his mane of brightly-coloured rags. One ear looked as if it might have been eaten by something, and he had a mouthful of large wooden teeth with which he gave wide, leering grins, which reminded Miss Minster of the off-side wheeler at Grasmere Town Head. His front legs pranced about nimbly, but the back legs tended to get left behind, occasionally trotting to catch up, and to trip over themselves at any sudden turn.

The Turkish knight wore smock and breeches like St. George, but had a very large, top-heavy turban, with a plume on the front shaped exactly like an old whitewash brush, fastened in place with a French revolutionary cockade. He was armed like St. George, but with a crescent on his shield. His face was black in patches, as if the cork which furnished his complexion had been imperfectly burned. His horse was similar to St. George's mount, but far less lively, with a distressing tendency for the back legs to lean against the front legs, as if it was tired.

The herald announced the play in a loud voice, interrupted by comments and guffaws from the audience, but, like most of the subsequent dialogue, the local dialect made it almost incomprehensible to the "offcomes".

The action of the play consisted mainly of a long-drawn-out battle between the two knights, interspersed with what were obviously fearful insults full of local jokes. St. George's visor tended to fall shut with a resounding clang whenever the Turkish knight hit him on the helmet with his wooden sword, and the turban fell off from time to time and had to be carefully replaced by the herald.

At length, St. George was dealt a mortal blow and lay a-dying on the floor. His horse galloped over, back legs staggering as the move took them unawares, and this was obviously an unexpected initiative from the front legs, which went down on their knees, leaving the back end sticking up in the air and inquiring what was going on in a piercing whisper. The head examined its master very carefully, and then the beast arose and chased the Turkish knight round and round the arena, teeth snapping furiously. The Turkish knight seemed a little surprised at first, but entered into the spirit of the chase, and ran with exaggeratedly high knee movements, rolling his eyes and blubbering loudly, to roars of delighted mirth from the audience, and the chase held up the action for some time.

Eventually, the back end of the horse fell over, and the herald hastily started on the traditional appeal for money to pay the doctor to heal St. George, and went round with a hat collecting coppers from the audience. Miss Minster recklessly threw in sixpence, and Sir Richard tossed in a generous quantity of small change. St. George was duly healed by a dose of medicine poured into him from a very large spoon, and his horse danced a celebratory jig with its front legs only, and then the battle was resumed until, after much thumping and thwacking, the Turkish knight was slain.

The hero of the fight stood in a suitable post, one foot on his fallen enemy, sword and shield held proudly, while the herald made a patriotic speech full of reference to the Corsican Monster, Our Gallant Soldiers and Sailors, and, in a neat little impromptu addition, especially Our Heroes of the Peninsula, with a bow to Sir Richard. Meanwhile, St. George's horse knelt down and started to eat the Turkish knight's turban, which was coming unswathed. Unfortunately, it proved to be poisoned, and after a little fierce whispering inside itself, the noble beast collapsed and died in agony, ending up in a curious position with its four legs more or less sticking up in the air, giving the herald an opportunity to take the hat round again!

When he had done so, Sir Richard said loudly that the best cure for a dead horse was a couple of pints of ale, and no doubt the same applied to dead Turkish knights and resurrected crusaders. He thanked the herald for his kind remarks about the Marquess of Wellington's Army in the Peninsula, and invited the cast to drink the Noble General's health at his expense. This was well received, especially by the slain, who recovered with remarkable alacrity. St. George's visor had fallen shut again, but he managed to get out of the helmet with a little help from his late mortal enemy, and shook Sir Richard by the hand, thanking him for his generosity and the loan of his servant. The Quality then left the room amid jovial good wishes, and returned to the parlour, where Sir Richard rang for tea, and Miss Minster firmly requested him to tell her how much she now owed him.

CHAPTER TWELVE

"THERE IS SOMETHING ELSE we must clear up first," he replied, but at that moment, the tea equipage arrived, and he begged Miss Minster to take her place at the table with teapot and cream jug first, as he was feeling excessively parched.

She sat down and set out the cups, and enquired how Mr. Tupper would like his tea, at which he sat down at the table and requested a little cream, put in *before* the tea. Sir Richard liked his much the same, but retired with it to stand by the fire, and waited until she had served herself and they had all drunk a little before saying, "Well, Mr. Tupper! We'd best set about it, I suppose."

"Ah. Well. Yes," Mr. Tupper replied, putting down his cup and adjusting his spectacles. "Will you, or shall I...?"

"You, I think, to begin with."

Miss Minster turned a puzzled and apprehensive gaze from Sir Richard to the solicitor, who cleared his throat and began, "I must beg that what I have to say shall remain confidential, as it might well be construed as damaging, although not slanderous, for it is certainly true."

"Of course it shall remain confidential," Miss Minster assured him, with difficulty as her lips and jaw seemed to have become very stiff.

"I happen to be fairly well acquainted with the Partridge family, you see, although, I hasten to add, not in professional capacity, in that they are not my clients, or, of course, I could not say anything about them."

Miss Minster nodded, feeling quite frightened of what was to come.

"Sir Marmaduke himself might, I think, be fairly described as high in the instep, unfriendly, very narrow in his views, and given to speaking contemptuously to and about his inferiors. He never has a good word to say about anyone, and he is forever taking on new servants, none of whom are contented, and they usually give notice as soon as may be. Your—er—predecessor did not even wait to do that, but left in a state of great indignation after only a month in his employ, for which, incidentally, he has refused to pay her, unfortunately with legal right on his side as she was in breach of contract, of course. I think I may best describe him as intolerant and lacking any consideration for others."

Mr. Tupper paused and looked at Sir Richard, who was drinking his tea and watching Miss Minster.

"Go on," she said in a small, tight voice, and Sir Richard nodded.

"Lady Partridge," Mr. Tupper resumed, "is a very proud, silly woman, with a shrill voice, a spiteful tongue, and much given to fits of the vapours. She barely condescends to acknowledge the existence of anyone of lower rank than herself. She is frequently ill, suffering, according to her—to a certain medical gentleman, from excessive spleen and boredom! She has never been known to express satisfaction about anything or anyone. The children, both girls, are much like her, and are extremely ignorant, largely because they must never be made to do anything they do not wish to do, but, of course, their parents blame it on the incompetence of the series of governesses who have come and gone over the years. No doubt you will feel I am exaggerating, but I fear I am not! I do not feel that I could possibly advise anyone to enter that household, particularly as an employee."

There was a silence for a few moments as Miss Minster considered what he had said, and also recalled a little more of Mr. Kirby's farewell speech. It seemed that her very worst fears were to be realised. She removed her gaze from Mr. Tupper's anxious face and automatically drank her tea, without any consciousness of what she was doing.

"Thank you for telling me," she said at length. "I shall not repeat anything of what you have said." She turned a little towards Sir Richard and said quite calmly, "May I have my note now, please?"

He took it from his cuff and limped to the table to put it down by her hand, then returned to the fireplace, putting his cup and dish on the mantelshelf. He looked very grave and concerned, but said nothing as she broke the seal and opened the note. After a quick glance at its contents, she gave a little sigh.

"You may be interested to hear what Sir Marmaduke has written," she said. Her voice was low and devoid of expression as she read aloud, "A conveyance was sent into Cockermouth to meet you on the 23rd of December, but you did not arrive as you had undertaken to do. However, the postmaster has assured one that it was impossible, in his opinion, for you to get here, in which case one will not hold you entirely responsible for your lateness. It is not convenient to send the gig..."

"Gig!" exclaimed Sir Richard. "An *open* carriage in this weather?"

"It is not convenient to send the gig again," Miss Minster continued, "but you may be able to hire a conveyance at your own expense, or, as it is no great distance for a young and healthy person, you may walk. Anyone will direct you, as it is a mere six miles. Any baggage you may have may be collected when there is an occasion at some time to send into town for purchases." She put the note down on the table, clasped her hands convulsively on top of it, and went quite white with distress.

"Well, that settles it!" Sir Richard said briskly. "You're not going there! I won't have it! Does that—that *idiot* really expect a lone female to *walk* six miles in this wilderness, in December?"

"Quite unreasonable! Typical, I fear!" Mr. Tupper commented. He shook his head and tut-tutted.

"I've nowhere else to go," Miss Minster said in what was meant to be a calm and reasonable manner. "I've only a few pennies left in the world. I owe you a great deal of money. I cannot pay my reckoning here, or even go back to Kendal. I've no other employment in prospect, and no means of living until I find something. I shall have to go there, and—and put up with it!" Her voice broke on a sob at the last words.

"You will not! You're coming with me to m'sister's!" Sir Richard said with great determination.

"But I owe you pounds already!" she exclaimed in great agitation, trying hard not to cry. "I'll never be free of debt to you if I take any more, and you can't just arrive at your sister's house with a strange woman!"

"Mr. Tupper, is it not true that a husband assumes responsibility for his wife's debts?" Sir Richard asked irrelevantly.

"He does not *assume*," the solicitor replied. "He *is* responsible for them unless he has publicly disclaimed that responsibility." He seemed disconcerted by this sudden red-herring.

"There's a solution, then!" said Sir Richard light-heartedly, but he was still watching Miss Minster with some anxiety.

"Oh, pray be careful!" Mr. Tupper cried agitatedly. "That could possibly be construed as an offer, you know, and before a witness, at that!"

Sir Richard gave him a remarkably cheerful and impish smile and said, "Could it now? Well, well! Call in the entire population of Cockermouth then, if it helps!"

Miss Minster looked at him for the first time since Mr. Tupper began his account of the Partridge family, but only with a dazed and puzzled non-comprehension.

"Come to m'sister's," he said coaxingly.

"Is she in need of a governess, then?"

"Not that I know of—unless she's breeding and ain't told me yet. You don't really want to be a governess all that much, do you?"

"What else can a respectable female of good family and no prospects do?" she asked bitterly.

"Well, she might marry 'a single man in possession of a good fortune' perhaps."

She still did not understand him, but replied with a twisted little smile, "Such an one would look for a Fortune or a Beauty, and I, unfortunately, am neither!"

"He might overlook that if he was not in the best of repair, and also happened to be very much in love with you. After all, a man who isn't in the pink of physical perfection can hardly expect more than a modest fortune—say about ninepence—particularly if the lady happens to have very beautiful eyes, and hair that curls naturally if she will let it."

Miss Minster turned a shade paler, if that was possible, and stared at him with eyes that seemed to have grown enormous. Her lips parted, and she said faintly, "You can't possibly have said what I thought you did! I must be dreaming!''

"I'm trying to ask you to marry me," he said patiently. "'Though I'm making heavy weather of it, I fear.'' As she still stared at him and said nothing, he went on a trifle desperately, "I shan't be so very lame when the wound is properly healed, but I'll admit I'll never dance again, and there'll always be a weakness there. I don't know if that matters to you or not."

"It's an offer I would most certainly advise you to accept, my dear young lady," Mr. Tupper said helpfully, and thereby caused confusion, for Miss Minster said, "Yes," very faintly.

"Er—forgive me if I appear obtuse," Sir Richard said breathlessly, "But in this context, do you mean 'yes, it does matter' or 'yes, you will marry me'?"

"No, I mean yes," Miss Minster blurted, then made an effort and pulled herself together. "I mean no, it doesn't matter, and yes, I will marry you, if you really want me, and I—I do love you so very much!" after which, she dissolved into tears.

Sir Richard let out his breath with an explosive sound and gathered her into his arms by the simple expedient of lifting her clear out of her chair, which fell over in the process, and begged her very earnestly not to cry, unless she particularly wished to do so, in which case she must do so on his shoulder, and that all her debts were cancelled because he couldn't cope with the high finance involved in owing money to himself, and in any case he couldn't bear to think she might feel obliged to marry him because she owed him money, and she must only accept him if she really wanted to, and a great deal of similar nonsense, but she silenced him eventually by raising her head from his now slightly damp gold braid to smile dazzlingly at him and assure him that she had been totally in despair at the thought of parting from him, for she loved him to distraction, which he seemed to find very satisfactory.

"Well, I think I'd best be making my way home," Mr. Tupper said benignly, smiling upon them. "It's growing late. Such a very satisfactory conclusion, if I may say so! Don't bother to say goodbye, for I'll come in the morning to see you off. I'll find my own way out. Goodnight!" He collected up his belongings from the Coromandel chest and tiptoed to the door, letting himself out and closing it behind him very quietly. He need not have bothered, for Sir Richard was kissing his Dorcas with passionate fervour, and neither of them was in the least conscious of his presence, his farewell speech, or his exit, being entirely absorbed in one another, to the exclusion of all else.

Some time later, Miss Minster recovered a semblance of consciousness of more mundane matters, placed her hands on the braided magnificence of her lover's chest, and levered herself far enough away from him to speak.

"But what shall I do about the Partridges?" she asked breathlessly.

Sir Richard smiled lovingly upon her, his eyes travelling about her face in a visual caress, as if he were selecting the place at which to begin his next series of kisses, and replied without hesitation, "Send Jem to 'em in the morning with a note to tell 'em you're not coming."

"But what reason shall I give?"

"Plead a subsequent engagement, and invite 'em to the wedding, if you like!" He was too happy to be out of charity with anyone, and did not grudge even the Partridges a slice of bridecake.

"And your sister?"

"Lucinda? Oh, she'll be busy organising your bride-clothes and trousseau—two dozen of everything takes some organising, you know! Besides, she'll have all those wallflowers to bed out somewhere else!"

"But when she finds you've only known me five days—whatever will she say?"

"That for once in my life, I've done something sensible! In any case, I've *known* you all my life—I just didn't *find* you until five days ago!"

"But . . ."

"Dearest nanny-goat! You're butting again!"

"But . . ."

He laughed, pulled her close again, and silenced her doubts very effectively.

POST-SCRIPTUM

30th. July, 1816

Lady Severall wrote the date at the top of a sheet of letterpaper, and then paused to brush the end of her pen against her lips and considered what she wished to write to her sister-in-law. It was difficult to concentrate, for the sun was shining outside, the bees were humming in the roses about the window of her little first-floor sitting-room, and it seemed quite wrong to be indoors on such a lovely day.

From her seat at her dainty Adam *bonheur du jour*, she could look down on the terrace at the back of the pleasant, mellow old house, and see the assortment of cats which lolled about in abandoned attitudes on the sun-soaked stone slabs which paved it, and a couple of her husband's spaniels waiting patiently for him to appear.

Below the terrace, on the neatly-mowed green lawn, Jem was engaged on losing an argument with a small grey donkey on a lunging-rein, which apparently objected to running round in circles, probably thinking it a very stupid activity on such a day, particularly as its friend, a larger brown donkey, was happily occupied behind Jem's back in eating its way through a large bush of red roses.

Beyond the lawn, some fine old trees framed a picturesque view of rolling Hampshire countryside, liberally set with thatched cottages, cows, sheep, smocked agricultural workers, and a neat little church, with a cloudless sky of improbable blueness over all. There was not a mountain or even a sizeable hill in sight, she was pleased to recall.

The dogs set up an excited yapping and attracted her attention back to the terrace, where her husband had just appeared and was standing admonishing the dogs to be a little quieter. He no longer walked with a stick, and had both arms occupied with carrying Master Arthur John Severall, aged exactly six weeks today, and named in honour of the great Duke. His second name had been selected by his father in remembrance of his maternal grandfather, which had been much appreciated by his mother.

Smiling, she got up from her chair, her pen rolling unnoticed across the paper, spattering ink, and went to the window to watch her son meeting the dogs and cats for the first time, and when Sir Richard looked up and called to her to join them, she left the room to run down to him without a second thought for her abandoned letter.

Harlequin Regency Romance™

COMING NEXT MONTH

#9 SWEET DORO by Dixie Lee McKeone

Finding herself in London for the Season is a great surprise to Lady Dorothea Sailings. Widowed for six years, she has been living in the country with her young charges, whom she has now reluctantly brought to London for a bit of town polish. But the real surprise is becoming reacquainted with Garreth Amberson, Viscount Tolver, who has also brought his ward to London for the first time. Although sixteen years have passed, Doro and Garreth agree to join forces "in the best interest of the youngsters," only to learn how little their own interest has changed.

#10 THE DEVIL'S DARE by Jean Reece

An unexpected accident brought Lord Dare to Elaine Farrington's rescue. Knowing Lord Dare to be called The Devil's Dare for his rakish ways and madcap pranks, Elaine resisted his persistent advances. Yet her brother, Nicholas, considered Dare a great gun. Consequently, Lord Dare was admitted to their home and hearth on a regular basis. In the meantime, Elaine learned that the Scottish Regalia was missing and that someone suspected it was secreted in her house. When threatening notes arrived and trespassers were detected, Elaine had to face the unpleasant truth. Who else but Lord Dare had unlimited access to her house? Who else but Lord Dare would accept a mission so devious? There was nothing for it. The man she had sworn never to love was a traitor to the English Crown.

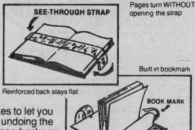